Deborah

drawings by

Joan Berg

Deborah

Bernice Hogan

New York Abingdon Press *Nashville*

Printed in the United States of America
Library of Congress Catalog Card Number: 64:10149

To Deborah,

my niece

Deborah

Chapter 1

Deborah dodged behind the blind beggars sitting by the weaver's stall and scrambled around the kneeling camel placidly chewing three whisks of straw.

If she could find her father quickly, maybe he would buy a special treat on this trip to Bethel. Always when their donkeys had lugged the bulging bundles of wool to market, and when Zelophad had gotten the best price on the market that day, Deborah would look longingly at the golden figs, the dark juice-oozing raisins, and the tempting pomegranates. What a feast they could have with these at home!

Deborah knew that her father was little interested in luxuries, but maybe this time he would take some honey for Tirzah to put in the wheat cakes. Maybe this time! So hopeful was she that she almost stumbled over an infant in the road busily stirring up dirt with his chubby fingers.

With a look of indignation, the child's mother snatched the baby up, but Deborah had already darted away, hurrying to Zelophad's side at one of the stall shops lining the crooked road.

"Zelophad, my cousin," an ancient wizened woman was whining, "such a good price for this metal tray! Upon this one Tirzah can bake her loaves more easily. Such a little money, Zelophad," she pleaded, rubbing her bony thumb over gnarled fingers in eager anticipation of a few shekels.

Deborah was fascinated by the glitter of the tray. In all her thirteen years she had never seen such trays in the tents of the Hebrews.

The father of Deborah showed little interest, however.

"These trays came from Harosheth. See how well those Canaanites work with metal—even if they don't know a ram from a goat!" The old woman cackled in a high-pitched laugh, thoroughly pleased with her joke on the hated Canaanites who worked so well with metals, yet knew so little of sheepherding.

Deborah pushed back her curly brown hair so that her headpiece, already mussed from her dash through the marketplace, slipped down to her shoulders. Cautiously she reached out her hand, and with her fingertips touched the shining metal tray in the old woman's lap.

If only her mother might have such a beautiful gift from the city!

Simeon, two years her junior, edged close now also, his eyes wide with amazement at the silvery pieces.

"Eeee-yah! Eeee-yah!"

From the noisy shuffle of the marketplace rose a snort and sound—shrill even above the usual bids and bargainings.

Eager for excitement and adventure, Deborah and Simeon

sped through the crowds at the first strange noise, though the sounds of the merchants and the selling of wares did not cease for a moment.

Zelophad, too, intrigued by the strange sound, ambled to find its source.

Darting over the sleepy camel this time, Deborah caught her breath as she saw a sleek black horse lying in the dust, snorting with anger and pain.

Above the animal stood a tall man with skin more bronze-colored than Deborah had ever seen before. His arms and legs were bare. His skin was darker than her own, yet with a ruddy glow about it. In his short blue tunic he stood defiantly over the stallion who was lying in the dust, pawing the earth with one foreleg in a vain attempt to rise. Again and again the man raised his whip above the frightened animal, and with vicious anger brought the leather thongs down upon the horse's back.

Two other men joined him now, their skins as bronze as the first, but with their own horses held tightly in harness lest they become skittish from the commotion.

Deborah glanced only sideways at the bronzed men in their short tunics, for she felt a sense of shame and embarrassment knowing that her own father and older brother Benjamin would never have entered a town with legs and arms bared.

The three men shouted to one another in a language Deborah could not understand, but she heard a shopkeeper, glaring with hatred at the foreigners, say to Zelophad, "Those Egyptians with their high-handed ways, I hate every one of them! That's a young stallion they're beating, and a proud one. He'd never get to his feet now—not with forty whips!"

Deborah cringed as the man with the blue tunic kicked the whinnying animal. She longed to run away from the cruelty, but she also wanted to help the handsome horse. Furtively she edged towards the Egyptian.

The animal snorted and writhed in pain. Blood ran over the sleek coat as the lashes from the whip cut deeper at each blow. Angrily the Egyptian pulled at the harness, but the horse's attempts to rise were now impossible.

Shouts from his companions finally distracted the tall man. He stopped the flaying of the whip and then, as if listening to their commands, gave a final kick to the horse's flank, and mounted behind the smaller of the two men. Without further hesitancy the two horses and their three riders sped off on the road northward towards Shechem.

Deborah watched the Egyptians depart. Swiftly then, she pulled off the headpiece, already fallen to her shoulders, and ran to the watering trough by the shop of Aaron the sandal-maker. Quickly she dipped the scarf in the tepid water, then pushed her way back through the crowd, now milling about their own businesses of buying and selling. Deborah squirmed and darted her way back to the fallen stallion.

Stooping quickly in the roadway by the horse, Deborah wiped at the blood on the handsome animal with her wet scarf. Her sharp brown eyes winced as the animal started with pain even at her gentle touches. The sight of the raw slashes made Deborah sick inside, but insistently she kept applying the wet scarf to the open wounds from the whip.

Merchants and traders of her own people now began forcibly to pull upon the horse to move it from the center of the dusty and well-traveled road. Zelophad helped push from behind as Aaron the sandalmaker urged the men to bring the animal over by his watering trough.

Deborah noticed, too, that now, Asahiah, third cousin of her mother, and the tallest man of all the tribe, as well as the fiercest looking with his flaming red hair, had also begun to pull upon the horse. Asahiah's son, Lapidoth, was there, too, but his tall angular body seemed to give little help in the moving of the animal for his eyes seemed lost in some cloud formation far past the sprawling tents and shops of Bethel.

It seemed strange to Deborah that Asahiah, wealthiest of all the tent dwellers, and well known for his shrewd bargainings, would concern himself over a fallen horse. It was not long, however, before she had the answer to her question. From his first words, Deborah could fathom the workings of this burly red-haired relative's mind.

"Horse is no good now. Probably will have to be killed," Asahiah said in a matter-of-fact voice to the men by the sandalmaker's shop.

Instinctively Deborah knew Asahiah had not the slightest intention of letting the horse be killed.

Zelophad shrugged his shoulders. He had enough problems

with his sheep and goats and three donkeys without worrying about a horse.

The mind of Aaron, however, had now begun to function and casting a sly look at the taller man, he asked, "You want to kill the horse, Asahiah?"

"I'll take care of the animal."

"Here in the shop?"

"I'll take care of it—elsewhere."

"But the horse is here now, on my property, so it is now mine. Suppose you were to take the horse, and it improved before you struck it a death blow. Then, my friend, Asahiah, you would possess my property, would you not?"

"No. I would possess the Egyptian's property."

"You are wrong. The horse is mine because it lies now upon my land."

Asahiah appraised his bargainer with a slight furrow of the eyebrows.

"Oh, yes, Aaron, I understand quite well that not one among us would so humiliate himself as to keep such an animal as this that the Egyptians used only for sport and to flaunt their luxury in our eyes."

Asahiah kicked some of the dust from the ground upon the horse as if he were wishing the dust were being swept into the eyes of the Egyptian strangers.

"On the other hand," Asahiah continued, "would it not help you, my brother Aaron, if I removed the worthless animal from your property, and at the same time found that my entire family suddenly needed three pairs of sandals of your making?"

"Five pairs of sandals *might* take care of the matter."

"I purchase four pairs and no more, and also rid you of killing the worthless beast."

Aaron nodded. Secretly he was delighted in having sold even four pairs of shoes for a horse he didn't own and whose masters he despised in the first place.

"Take care of the horse, Lapidoth," Asahiah said to the tall son beside him. "We won't kill him this day!"

"Perhaps tomorrow," he added winking at Zelophad.

Asahiah walked towards the street, then turned and looked at his only son.

"The horse is yours, Lapidoth, if you can forget your dreaming long enough to care for its needs. A sick horse may be worthless, but should it be healed under your care. There are those who would pay handsomely for it. It may be only a luxury for the Egyptians, and sneered upon when it is even seldom seen by our people, but for me, Asahiah, I do not care. I am one for a shrewd bargain—whether it be sheep or goats or even an Egyptian horse."

Deborah, listening from the corner of the stall, wondered what the tribespeople would say about Asahiah bringing a pagan animal to their camp.

Asahiah turned toward the sandalmaker, "I shall call for the shoes within a few days, Aaron."

Triumphantly the burly man left the shop well pleased with the business of the day.

"Come, Deborah," said Zelophad, touching his daughter briskly on the shoulder. "We must be back to the tents before sundown."

"So this is Deborah," said the sandalmaker to Zelophad. "Strange, I have never seen a girl care so gently for an animal—much less an Egyptian horse. Deborah, indeed, I am going to remember that name!"

At the words of praise, Deborah could feel the flush of embarrassment rise in her face and spread backward to her ears when another voice interrupted. Lapidoth the son of Asahiah was saying quietly, "Your kindness is very great, Deborah."

Deborah's face had now become scarlet. How glad she was when suddenly Simeon appeared in the doorway dangling a strip of leather excitedly.

"Look what I found! It came from the Egyptian's horse. It's part of the harness. Look how smooth the leather is! See the scroll designs on the edge; I have never seen such fine work. I'm taking it home to show Benjamin and the boys."

Deborah looked at the small piece of leather. It didn't seem to be anything to be so excited over, but she knew how Simeon longed to do fine work with his hands. He was only eleven, but Deborah could not remember a time when Simeon was not painstakingly carving a piece of wood or polishing a bright colored stone.

"Deborah, see what a mess your scarf is in! You'd surely better clean that up before Mother sees it," warned Simeon.

Deborah looked at the mantle with dismay. It *was* a mess!

Deliberately she walked to the well at the end of the street, and absentmindedly drew out the water. Rubbing the scarf between her hands, she thought how Aaron despised the Egyptian horse. If Aaron, who lived in Bethel and saw such foreign things often, felt this way—what could Asahiah be thinking of by taking the horse back to their camp?

"Deborah! Come on! Father is ready to leave now!"

Zelophad had already sold the wool from their sheep in the marketplace and he had no interest in dawdling over a sick pagan horse.

"Come on, Deborah, I'll race you to the donkeys," cried Simeon.

Deborah's legs were longer than Simeon's, but she was lost in thought, and they moved less swiftly today.

"Deborah, you are a slowpoke," taunted Simeon who had already thrown himself down in the dust by the donkeys. "We will never get home if you walk so slowly! I want to show this harness strap to Benjamin and the boys. Deborah, I could do this, if only I had the tools, I know I could."

Simeon's enthusiasm brought Deborah out of her thoughts.

"It is a beautiful piece of work, Simeon. Perhaps Benjamin will help you fashion tools with which you can work leather. You are lucky to have a brother like Benjamin who not only understands your interest in such things, but is clever too."

As the trio bounced along the dusty road, Zelophad glanced anxiously at the sky. Storm clouds hovered in the south in the direction of their tents.

Simeon happily chanted a familiar song of praise, but Deborah did not join in the singing. She was too bewildered by her own feelings. On the one hand, she felt pain from watching the writhing of the great horse in its terrible suffering, and yet she did not see how Asahiah and Lapidoth could keep it.

She watched Simeon proudly swing the leather strap about his hand, and then, as it suddenly reminded her of her own present problems, Deborah smoothed out the wet and wrinkled scarf. If she let it hang loosely over her shoulders, perhaps it would dry enough so that Tirzah would not see the dark stains and frayed edges quite so quickly.

Chapter 2

The sky was black, and smoky gray clouds ominously hovered over the tents, as Zelophad and his children approached their homes. The ground was damp as if some rain had already fallen, yet the moisture seemed to have been almost swallowed up by the arid ground.

"Where can Tirzah be?" muttered Zelophad.

"Look, Father. Over there where the women are standing!" Deborah cried eagerly.

Tirzah was in the midst of the women who were all talking at once, giving no heed to what anyone else was saying. There was no danger of a wrinkled and torn scarf being noticed amid this excitement. Deborah strained to see what had caused such commotion.

Thunder rumbled, and the donkeys stopped in nervous caution.

"Here, Simeon, you care for these animals," cried Zelophad, as he hurried toward the group of agitated women.

Seeing her husband approaching, Tirzah left her kinswomen,

and came toward her husband wringing her hands together with worry and distraction.

"Zelophad, look at this awful thing that has happened to us. The great thunder clouds gathered, and when the storm finally broke, the fierce and angry lightning flashed about the tents of all of us. Some of the tents were even upset from the winds, but that is not the worst of the storm. Look, Zelophad, look at that great tree!"

Zelophad edged his way in among the women, and Deborah, too, crowded close behind her father.

There, sprawled across the ground, was a sycamore tree, its trunk broken and splintered by the lightning flash. The slivers stuck out like thin knives and sharp wooden daggers, warning the onlookers not to approach too closely.

"It is the hand of Yahweh pointing his finger in anger against us," spoke one woman in an almost hushed voice.

"God is surely displeased with us," nodded old Sarah, grandmother of Lapidoth.

Tirzah stood close by her husband and shivered in the dampness after the storm.

"We have surely committed a grave sin for God to warn us by destroying this strong tree."

"Yes," said the devout Zelophad, "Yahweh indeed is admonishing us to remember that he alone is God and greater than all our tribes. As he has struck down this tree, so he would admonish us that we also can be struck down by the might and power of his hand."

The women nodded, and looked uncomfortably about them. Was there one certain person of their tribe against whom this warning from God had been directed? Had one of their sycamore tree that their people would know of his anger?

Deborah looked at the tree lying upon the ground; the storm clouds still hovered in the sky above them. Was Yahweh really in those storm clouds? Had he really split the trunk of the sycamore tree that their people would know of his anger and warning?

Her father said it was true, and all the women about the spot surely believed that the lightning was the loud voice of God. How mighty, marveled Deborah, must God be to command those great clouds and the strong trees that snapped and were broken at the very movement of his fingers! It made her feel very small in the presence of this mighty Yahweh.

Still thinking about the fallen tree, Deborah wandered to the edge of the tribespeople. Looking away from the crowd she suddenly saw two familiar figures jogging upon their donkeys toward the tents.

The redness of Asahiah's hair could be recognized now, and Deborah could see Lapidoth beside his father. But the stallion, where was it? Surely they would have brought the horse back from Bethel if Lapidoth were to keep the animal.

Zelophad, too, had now seen Asahiah approaching, though the burly man's anger was already in evidence as he was heard growling at the donkeys for their disinterest in anything faster than a slow plodding gait.

"Asahiah," Zelophad called out to his kinsman, "and where's that heathen beast you were so determined to have? Don't tell me you traded him back to the Egyptians already?"

Asahiah grunted, "Horse is dead."

"The horse is dead!" gasped Deborah, looking at Lapidoth for some clearer reply.

"Yes," said Lapidoth, "the stallion must have been more badly hurt than we had thought, but it was strange nonetheless. He could not move rapidly when we left Bethel, and then a great storm of thunder and lightning and heavy rain met us as we were midway here. There were loud claps of thunder and sharp, fierce strokes of lightning. I thought one streak of lightning came directly toward us—it was as if it went straight through the stallion. He fell down, and when I reached him, he was not breathing anymore."

"Ridiculous," growled Asahiah, "the lightning never struck the stupid animal. He just fell down and died, just plain died, all by himself. He'd have died if there'd never been a storm—wouldn't have been of any use to me anyhow. It's better that he's gone!"

Asahiah thrust out his chest and walked about, looking at the tree, but Deborah's sharp eyes noted the uneasiness and worry in the nervous pacing of the man.

She looked questioningly at Lapidoth, still standing beside her. He had, she knew, some clearer knowledge of the trip from Bethel to the tents.

"It was the lightning, Deborah, I'm sure of that."

"But if lightning is the voice of God, as the women here are so sure in the falling of this tree, what does it mean, Lapidoth?"

"Who knows? Perhaps it was God punishing us for having taken the pagan animal; perhaps it was a punishment for something we did some other day or some other year. I do not know, Deborah. I cannot always understand the might and power of Yahweh, even though I worship him and bow down before him. It is strange. Yes, indeed it is very strange—the ways and the voice of the Lord."

"What are you doing now, Deborah?" said Simeon, whacking his sister soundly on the shoulder. "Come on now, let's go and see whether Benjamin and the other shepherds have come back with the flocks. Hurry up and stop talking so we can go and meet them."

Deborah felt a little annoyance at the interruption by her younger brother. She wanted to talk further with Lapidoth. Her mind had been plagued with questions since they had left Bethel, but seeing that Lapidoth was already moving off toward his father, Deborah gave Simeon a look of resigned disgust, and said finally. "All right, let's go and tell Benjamin about all that has happened today."

Simeon started in the direction the men had taken the sheep that morning, but Deborah raced ahead of him. She stopped suddenly and called back to him.

"Come on, Simeon, I'll race you to the sheepfold!"

"You'll never win, Deborah. I'll be there long before you have even started!"

"You think so, little brother? We shall see about that!"

Quickly the two began to run, but Deborah was alert now and her long legs carried her swiftly and gracefully. Simeon found it difficult even to keep close to his older sister.

"Come on, Simeon, I thought you would be at the sheepfold by now!" called out the tall girl.

But as Deborah turned to call out to Simeon, she stepped in a deep rut in the ground and fell sprawling to the ground. Deborah felt a sharp stab of pain piercing through her right ankle and leg.

"Deborah, what happened?"

Simeon was there immediately. He stooped down to help, then awkwardly tried to help her rise, but Deborah felt the pain mounting in her leg. She put her hands down to her ankle. She could already feel the swelling begin.

"Get Mother, Simeon," the girl cried. "She can help. She always knows what to do."

But as the boy rose to go, Deborah grabbed hold of his arm.

"No, Simeon, maybe we shouldn't worry Mother just now. Here, you help me back to the tent. Then you can go and get her so she won't be worried or frightened to see me here."

Painfully and slowly, Deborah inched her way to their own tent, leaning heavily on Simeon's shoulder.

Strangely, at each hurting step, Deborah wondered if the pain of the handsome stallion had been much greater than hers. Perhaps it was better that the horse, so foreign and strange to all of them, was dead.

Grasping the posts of her own tent door, she sank down upon the mat inside. Her head seemed to be whirling from the events of the day and her ankle throbbed agonizingly. She lay back for a moment on the straw mat.

It seemed to Deborah that in the distance she could hear Simeon calling for their mother, but now for her everything was dark and black and fading away.

It was daylight when Deborah finally and hesitantly opened her eyes. The tent poles seemed to swing before her, and her bed felt as if it were slipping away. Tirzah, her mother, kneeled close beside her, holding a goatskin pouch of water against her lips. The ankle still thobbed with pain.

"Deborah, are you awake?"

It was Simeon's voice, coming from the curtain at the women's side of the tent. Deborah half-turned her face away. Today nobody could make her forget the pain in her foot and leg.

"Look, Deborah, I know how your ankle hurts—really bad, I bet, but, look here, I've tried to make you something to forget your leg."

From behind his back, Simeon drew out a wooden flute and handed it to his sister.

"Got up early and made it myself. You always said you wanted a flute. Now you can learn to play while your ankle gets better. It's pretty smooth, if I say so myself—*almost* as smooth as my Egyptian harness."

Even with the pain, Deborah had to smile at the comparison

with the harness. But Simeon was right. He had made the flute well, and she noticed that the etchings in the wood were very similar to the leather designs on the strap. Slowly she picked up the carefully whittled instrument and placed the holes to her lips.

It *was* beautiful, in spite of the soreness of her leg.

Maybe the herbs Tirzah was now wrapping on her ankle would take the pounding away, but Simeon had been right, the flute did help to take her mind away from the pain.

Two shrill notes of music sounded through the tent, as Deborah blew tentatively into the reedlike instrument.

Deborah looked proudly at Simeon as he laughed, and Tirzah smiled gently at her two younger children.

Leaning back, then, on the mat and looking through the crack between the curtains, Deborah could see her father Zelophad and her older brother, Benjamin, sitting on the floor of the tent by the round straw mat, eating the bread baked so carefully by Tirzah the day before, and drinking the warm goat's milk.

With another glance at her daughter's leg, Tirzah slipped through the curtains to wait upon the needs of her husband and elder son. Simeon, too, had decided that even flute music was not so important as food, and he also slipped into his place about the round dining mat.

Holding tightly to her flute, Deborah closed her eyes and thought about her family. Her family was healthy and happy in spite of the frequent scarceness of food and uneasiness in the presence of their enemies in this land of Canaan where they dwelled. She was very proud that hers was a Hebrew family, that they were part of Yahweh's own chosen people. Her mind wandered to thoughts of last year when almost all their tribe had made the great trip to Shechem to worship in the tabernacle and to offer sacrifices to the Lord there before the Ark of the Covenant.

Even though she had been a girl and had had to remain far back with her mother and the younger Simeon in the women's outer court of the tent of the tabernacle, it had been a thrilling and exciting trip. No wonder their Lord was so great, when Deborah felt she could almost feel him right there before all of them in the courtyard of the tabernacle. How even more awed must Zelophad and the other men have felt when they could move at least a little closer to the holy of holies, the great Ark of the Covenant, which their people had brought through their wanderings in the deserts. How great and mighty was this Lord of their people! No wonder he seemed able to speak in the voice of the thunder and to reach out his hand with the lightning's flash.

Thinking about such things, the girl was becoming more sure than ever that the pain in her leg did not matter so much after all.

With her hand loosening upon the flute and her ankle still uncomfortable, Deborah again fell asleep.

Chapter 3

As the days passed the swelling of the ankle remained, but the herbs Tirzah persistently applied seemed to take away the pain, though every movement brought increased soreness to the leg.

Deborah was annoyed with herself for being helpless at such an exciting time. It was springtime, and the whole tribe was preparing for the observance of the Passover. The men had gone out among the flocks a few days before, and each had chosen an unblemished male lamb in its first year and had taken them to their tents to be kept until the eve of the Passover. This morning, Deborah had watched her father and Benjamin as they built the altar of stones on which the lamb would be sacrificed when the sun set and the Passover began.

In other years, Deborah had enthusiastically worked with Tirzah to prepare for the feast days. There was so much to do. The herbs to be eaten with the lamb had to be gathered. The tent had to be cleaned and all the leavening used in baking removed. The matzoh had to be baked on the smooth stones in the oven shared by many of the families of their tribe. Deborah fretted that she could do only those things that could be done as she lay upon her mat.

In spite of her discomfort, Deborah helped Tirzah mix the meal with oil, and carefully patted the mixture into flat, round loaves. Then, while Tirzah took the bread to the oven, Deborah prepared the herbs that Tirzah had gathered earlier. As she worked she thought of the many sufferings of her people.

They had been slaves in Egypt, and greatly oppressed. At one time the Pharaoh had feared the Hebrew slaves would become too numerous and strong, and had ordered all the male babies slain. Deborah thought of the baby that would soon be born to Tirzah. "If we were living then, and if the baby were to be a boy . . ." Deborah shivered at the horror of her thought. But one Hebrew baby was saved by his mother. The mother of Moses had hidden him among the bulrushes where the Pharaoh's daughter bathed. When the Egyptian princess found the baby Moses, she adopted him as her son, and he was raised as a prince of Egypt. It was the baby Moses who grew up to hate the misery that the Hebrew people suffered.

Tirzah had returned, but Deborah was so lost in her thoughts that she didn't notice. For a time Tirzah did not speak, and then, as though she sensed Deborah's thoughts, she said, "This bread is the same that our people had to eat on their journey to Canaan. When Yahweh commanded Moses to lead the Hebrew people out of Egypt, there was no time to add leavening to their bread to make it rise. Yahweh has commanded us to remember the days when he brought us out of Egypt by celebrating the Feast of the Unleavened Bread. Tonight is the Passover, the first night of the feast. And this night and for six days following we must eat nothing with leavening in it. The herbs you are preparing for us to eat with the lamb are very bitter—to remind us of the misery of our people while they were slaves in Egypt. On the seventh day of the feast we again do no work, but celebrate it as a holy day, as Yahweh commanded. You must remember these things, Deborah, for someday you will have a daughter of your own who must be taught to make the bitter herbs and the matzoh."

Simeon came into the tent now, carrying the lamb. It was sundown, and the Passover had begun.

Sitting on the straw mat with her injured leg stretched out before her, Deborah wondered how the Hebrews so many, many years before must have felt when the angel of death had passed over the homes of their people in Egypt. The Egyptians had refused to let the Hebrews go with Moses, and Yahweh had brought a plague to all the firstborn in Egypt. If the Lord saw the blood from the unblemished lamb upon the doorposts and lintels of a home, he knew it was a Hebrew home, and the angel of death "passed over" and the oldest child of the family was not killed.

Deborah's eyes grew wide in awe, as each year she saw her father take the hyssop branch and smear the blood from their own lamb upon the tent posts in remembrance of the Hebrews having been spared by the angel of death.

The slain lamb was placed whole upon the stones and slowly roasted. Tirzah was close beside her now, and Simeon, Benjamin, and Zelophad had all gathered within the tent. They had sandals on their feet, and the men had staffs in their hands. They seemed about ready to depart on a journey. For this was the manner in which they ate the Passover meal, in haste, as had their people on the first Passover. The feeling of remorse that Deborah felt because she must lie upon a mat was quickly forgotten as the service began.

"What is the meaning of this service?" asked Simeon.

Zelophad stood proud and tall as he gave the answer known to every Hebrew and told by the head of every household on the Passover night.

"It is because of what the Lord did for me when I came out of Egypt. By strength of hand the Lord brought us out of Egypt, from the house of bondage. For when Pharaoh stubbornly refused to let us go, the Lord slew all the firstborn in the land of Egypt, both the firstborn of man and the firstborn of cattle. Therefore I sacrifice to the Lord all the males that first open the womb; but all the firstborn of my sons I redeem. 'And this day shall be unto you for a memorial, ye shall keep it a feast to Jehovah: throughout your generations he shall keep it a feast by an ordinance for ever.' "

As the lamb roasted, Zelophad told the stories of their people that had been told to him by his father, and by his father's father. Deborah listened to her father telling now of Jacob's wonderful experience at Bethel. It seemed to Deborah that she could almost see Jacob with his head upon the pillow of stone and the angels treading up and down the ladder of his dreams.

Zelophad's telling of the old stories seemed so real to Deborah that she wept for Jacob when her father told of Joseph, Jacob's favorite and youngest son, and how his jealous brothers sold him to Egyptian slave traders. But Joseph won the favor of the Pharaoh, Zelophad went on, and when famine came to Canaan, all Israel went down into Egypt where they were allowed to dwell in peace because they were Joseph's people.

"How brave and wise Joseph must have been," marveled Deborah, as she thought how Israel and Egypt both might have starved during the famine had it not been for Jacob's son.

Zelophad's voice became lower now, and Deborah thought it tremored with sadness as he continued.

"But Joseph died, and generations passed, and a new king arose over Egypt who did not know Joseph. The new king made slaves of the people of Israel, and from then on, all the years our people were in Egypt were filled with cruelty, and bitterness, and hardship."

Benjamin now took up the storytelling, and he related how Yahweh had commanded Moses to bring Israel out of Egypt, and how they had wandered in the wilderness for many years before reaching the promised land. Deborah always felt a great wave of relief when the story finally reached Joshua's leading the Hebrews to this, their own land of Canaan, the land that God had promised would be "milk and honey" indeed.

Vaguely, Deborah wondered to herself how this land of "milk and honey" could be so dry, how it could have so many rocks and ruts, and so very many enemies of their people.

The hour was growing late and the lamb was ready to be eaten.

As they ate, Deborah wondered why the Canaanites fought so fiercely against the Hebrews, trying constantly to push them out of all the land of Canaan.

"Why, Benjamin," Deborah had been asking one day when several of their sheep and goats had been killed by nearby

Canaanites, "why don't they want us near their farms and towns? We're only looking for better grazing land and more water for our sheep."

"The Canaanites are not like our people," Benjamin had said that day. "They do not worship Yahweh, and they have many idols and images of their many gods. They do not like us because our God, Yahweh, forbids us to do many things that they do. We will not worship their gods, and we must follow the Commandments that Yahweh gave to Moses. Father says he has heard that much evil goes on in the great northern Canaanite cities like Harosheth and Megiddo. Perhaps it is because we do not live as they do, that they dislike us."

But on the Passover she should not be thinking of such things as enemies, Deborah reminded herself. This was the time for all of them to feast together on the lamb they had offered as a sacrifice. All night they would eat of the roasted lamb, but in the morning all the meat left from the sacrifice must be destroyed. This was the Passover law, and would be carried out by every loyal Hebrew.

The feast days passed all too quickly, it seemed to Deborah. The week of Unleavened Bread was almost past; tonight at sundown the last day would begin. The men had already begun bringing the flocks close to the camp, and the women had prepared enough food to last through the following day, for this last day of Unleavened Bread was a holy day, and no work could be done.

Deborah could be up and walk haltingly outside around the tent. How sore her ankle still seemed, and how strangely stiff. The out-of-doors had never seemed so lovely, and now, after having been confined for so long, the hills surrounding the camp seemed to be calling to her to come and explore the wonders on their gentle slopes.

Just as she was beginning to feel sorry for herself, Deborah saw Zelophad and Benjamin coming toward the camp.

"Surely I can at least walk well enough to meet them," Deborah thought to herself, and began to hobble toward her father and brother.

"Ah, Deborah," said Benjamin, as she drew close to them, "it is good to see that your leg is better."

Zelophad strode on ahead, and Benjamin slowed his step so that Deborah could keep up with him.

"Father is worried, Deborah. Each day we have been having to go farther and farther from the tents to find sufficient grass for the sheep. There is talk among the tribe that perhaps we should move again soon. The time for the baby to come is soon, and Father is afraid for Tirzah and the child if she must do all the work of moving without you to help her."

"He need not worry so, Benjamin. I am walking much better now, and there is Simeon to help. Even so, must we move so soon? It would be better if we waited until after the baby is born."

"Yes, but the sheep must be kept fed and watered, too. We will see; the men will decide. Come, little one, the sun is setting, and Father would be angry to hear us discussing work on a holy day."

Deborah wondered if the concern for grazing land and water were the only reason the men were in such a hurry to move again. In between conversations about their sheep and goats, Deborah had heard the men talk of other dangers. She had seen Asahiah shaking his fist in the air just yesterday, and shouting about the heathen Canaanites who had robbed him of all chance of building up his flocks with their frequent thievery. Perhaps now the men feared an attack upon their own tent people.

Deborah followed Benjamin inside the tent, and the family sat around the dining mat and began the meal that marked the seventh day of the Feast of the Unleavened Bread.

Deborah could not keep her mind on the stories and songs. She could see the worry in her father's eyes, though he would never admit such fear to the women of his family. Deborah felt that Tirzah saw it too, but she knew Tirzah would say nothing. She was a woman, and had no authority, so for the sake of her children she would pretend not even to know about the uneasiness of the shepherds.

Two days later the men again took the flocks to the hills. "We will not go far," Benjamin had told Deborah, "the men have decided that we must move soon."

When the men were gone, Tirzah called Deborah and Simeon to her. "We must prepare to move the tents. Today, while your father and brother are with the sheep, we will sort our possessions—then there will not be so much to do when the men return."

Even though the family had few possessions, and they were used to moving, there was much to be done. It took them most of the day. Though her leg was stronger now, Deborah still limped, and this slowed her somewhat.

"It's almost sundown," Simeon came into the tent to report. "Why have Father and Benjamin not yet come home?"

"They will soon be here," Tirzah said calmly, setting down the water jugs in the coolest portion of the tent. "All is well, they will soon be here."

Her voice never wavered, but her eyes seemed doubtful and uncertain.

"Deborah, why don't we walk to the top of the hill, and see if we can see the flocks coming home?" Simeon suggested restlessly.

Deborah hesitated. Perhaps there was more she ought to be doing for Tirzah, but her mother motioned her off.

"Go on to the top of the hill with Simeon. You'll be able to see Father from there by now, I know. Go, Deborah, all is ready here now, and the meal is prepared."

Deborah noted that the climb up the hill did not hurt her leg as much as it had earlier.

"It's strange that we can't see the men and the flocks from here," said the girl as they stood looking out over the valley.

"The sun's almost setting, Deborah," Simeon said, pointing

to the fiery red ball almost hidden now behind some farther hills. "The men have never before been so late."

"Surely, they would not stay out in the fields past sundown," reasoned Deborah, uncertain herself of the dread and fear that began to grip her heart.

"They said they would be back. They told us to prepare to move the tents—I know something has happened to change their plans, Deborah, I know it."

Deborah sought for words to reassure him, but she knew what he said was all too true.

"I'd like to go and look for them, Deborah. Would you go with me?"

"But Simeon, what would Mother say?"

"You know very well what she'd say, 'Simeon is the baby; Simeon is too young.' Why does everyone always think I'm too young to help?"

Stooping down he picked up a stone and hurled it across the dry dirt, kicking up a small spray of dust with the force.

"We've got to do something," Simeon urged impatiently. "Father and Benjamin may be in danger. We have to help, Deborah. You go and ask Mother if we can't at least go and look for them."

"Hush, Simeon. You mustn't let Mother see you so angry and upset. Besides, you have been helping Mother and me all day—no one says you are too young to be of help."

"Woman's work! I want to do something that really matters."

"We shall see," said Deborah. "I will talk with Mother after the evening meal. Perhaps she will let us get an early start tomorrow morning—but surely they will have returned by then!"

Deborah stood up and turned her right leg with care, for the stiffness still prevented rapid movement. Looking out over the valley, she saw the grass sparse and dry. When they had moved here with the tribe her father had been certain that the wells would be full and the rains plentiful, but the single well had almost dried up now and not a cloud seemed to promise rain.

Water and grass, food and water, grass and food—this she had heard in a constant cycle all of her life. Seldom had there really been enough of any of them, yet all their tribes kept on searching. How could the Canaanites, Deborah wondered, resent their search for good land and food and water when they, the Hebrews, needed such things so badly?

"In the name of Baal and Astarte, why are you dawdling so long? We've got to work to do, if we're going to leave tomorrow morning!"

"For shame, Simeon," reprimanded Deborah, "using the names of Canaanite gods! Yahweh will surely punish you for such disobedience!"

As they neared their own tent, they could see Tirzah measuring out the epah of meal for the next day's baking of bread. Carefully every day she took three seahs of meal and mixed it with salt, some of the precious water and the yeast dough left from the baking of the day before. Then Tirzah would put the dough in the common kneading trough nearby that was shared by several of the families, and this was work for the early morning hours, although at least the meal would be measured for the morrow.

"Mother, have you had news from Father or Benjamin?" Deborah asked in a voice that only partly hid her fear and anxiety.

"They will come, my daughter. Surely they will come soon."

"But the other women, Mother, what do they say? Haven't they heard any news either? I can see that many of the men and most of the flocks have not come back today."

Instantly Deborah regretted the tenseness of her voice, but Tirzah seemed not to notice.

"There is no news, only rumors that the Canaanites are moving closer to our flocks and may try to drive us further south out of these hills."

"Maybe Father and Benjamin will be here by sundown," suggested Simeon, squatting down near his mother and sister.

The sun had already passed over the rim of the hill when the three spread out the round straw mat for eating.

"We will save these extra loaves for Father and Benjamin," said Tirzah, also putting aside her own bread, for fear had snatched away her appetite.

"Tonight, I will be the man of the family and sit by the fire until the others return," said Simeon with an enthusiasm he little felt.

"And I will sit with you," added Deborah, "for surely it will not be long until they are back."

Tirzah nodded. It would not be for her to sleep either, but she would gather her fear to herself and stay within the tent.

"Mother," Deborah asked cautiously, "may Simeon and I go to look for the men tomorrow?"

"We will be most careful. We *can* be of help, Mother, I know we can," begged Simeon moving closer and putting his arms pleadingly over his Mother's shoulders.

Tirzah looked at her two children. Deborah saw the well-concealed worry in her eyes.

"Perhaps," said Tirzah as she pulled the tent flap behind her heavy body and entered the dark room.

Outside Simeon was now full of eagerness and anticipation for the excitement of the next day as he dashed back and forth gathering more sticks for the fire and spreading out his cloak by the side of it.

"Here, Deborah," he offered, spreading out his sister's cloak for her in an unusual demonstration of good nature, "let's make ourselves comfortable by the fire for the rest of the night."

"We will not have to wait long, for Father and Benjamin may come at any moment," insisted Deborah, although she knew that travel by night with the flocks was almost impossible over such rough country.

"They will surely be here before daybreak."

"Yes, yes. I am sure you are right, Deborah!" answered Simeon, furtively fingering the Egyptian leather strap he continually wore looped over his tunic belt.

There was little assurance in either of their voices.

Chapter 4

When Deborah awoke, the sun was rising now over the Judean hills, and she moved her leg stiffly under the cloak Simeon had thrown over her during the night.

Suddenly she sat upright.

How could she have forgotten, even for a moment, about Benjamin and her father!

"Simeon," she called, seeing her younger brother already wrapping in a cloth the bread loaves not eaten the night before. "Is there any news? Did anyone come home last night?"

"Nothing's changed. No one has come, but at least Mother has said that we can go today."

They could see Tirzah by the well talking with the other women, and Deborah noticed how difficult it was for her mother to lift the water jugs, and how awkwardly she made her way back to their tent. It would not be long now until Tirzah's fourth child would be born. Deborah knew that her mother must stay with the women of the tribe, in spite of her desperate concern for Zelophad and Benjamin.

Tirzah came closer to Simeon and Deborah now, and her eyes had deep tenderness in them as she clasped the two children impetuously to her.

"May the Lord be with your going out and your coming back this day, and may no harm come unto our family or unto our people according to our obedience unto the Lord, our God."

Reluctantly Tirzah released her son and daughter from the embrace and awkwardly went into the tent and lay down upon the straw mat.

"Come, Deborah, we must go now," urged Simeon. "We must hurry if we are to find Father and Benjamin."

Deborah moved hesitantly to the doorway of the tent, torn between the desire to comfort her mother and to search for her father. Tirzah, seeing the girl in the doorway, motioned for her daughter to go on.

With a worried backward glance, Deborah picked up the packet of small bread loaves and a goatskin filled with water. Then, with a quick look about, she also picked up a short wooden stick—what would they need today? she wondered.

Simeon held a wooden shepherd's staff with a crooked end that could reach out and pull back the sheep wandering too close to a precipice. It was a tall staff, really too large for the young Simeon, yet its size and the feel of the wood, worn smooth by his father's hand, gave him a feeling of courage and manliness. All his life, Simeon could remember Benjamin and their father carrying this staff or another shaped just like it.

Along the side of the hill, the boy and girl now made their

way in the direction toward which the men had left two days before. They could look back and see their tent, but the sight so filled them with fear and uncertainty that both were tempted to run back to Tirzah for comfort and security.

Deborah raised her chin abruptly and said with seeming confidence, "Come, Simeon, we must walk more quickly. See, even the flocks which I saw grazing here yesterday have now gone."

Simeon quickened his steps to keep up with his sister. The sun rose higher and became hotter, its glare grew more intense.

They seldom spoke, for fear of the unknown grew more paralyzing in their hearts. In all these hills around Mount Ephraim, how could they ever find their father and brother? Neither dared to suggest that perhaps they should not have come in the first place.

They had reached the lower valley some distance below where the tribe was settled. No familiar tent could be seen now, but at least here there was a dirt road on which they could more easily make their way.

"Look at the strange markings in the road, Deborah. Who do you think has come by here recently?"

"These small tracks are from many donkeys, I think, Simeon, but these wide straight ones, I am not sure about," answered Deborah, moving the loose dirt away from the markings with her foot.

"Perhaps there were oxen here pulling a large cart," suggested Simeon.

"Yes, yes, that must be right," replied Deborah, not in the least convinced that Simeon's suggestion was correct.

The road did make travel quicker and easier, and Deborah kept her eyes on the hills in the distance. It was always to the north that the men traveled when seeking better grazing lands. Surely on one of those ledges or near one of those not-so-far-off hills, Zelophad and Benjamin would be found.

"They *will* be safe, Simeon, I am sure of it. Father and Benjamin and the other men live so carefully by the laws of the Lord. It is never they who worship idols or false gods. Our family obeys Yahweh, and I am certain that the Lord will not forsake us now when we need him."

"I will be glad when I am old enough to stand with the men in the tent of the congregation when we make our journey to the tabernacle at the Feast of the Ingathering," yearned Simeon with eleven-year-old wistfulness. "I know I could make a good sacrifice to the Lord, and I would be glad to give him the very best of everything I possess. If only I were old enough now to give something to Yahweh!"

A distant rumbling halted Simeon's wishing, and the two stopped suddenly to look southward.

"Something big is coming!" cried Deborah, pulling Simeon with her behind some bushes by the edge of the road.

"Look, Deborah, look!"

"Down, Simeon, stay down!"

"It is here!" hissed Simeon raising his dark hair above the bushes for a better look.

"Stay down, Simeon. Whoever is coming is certainly not of our people. Be very still and perhaps they will not be able to see us!"

The rumbling increased and the dust of the road was thrown up in great clouds as the children peered through the leaves of the bushes.

"It's a chariot, Deborah. I can see now. I'm sure it's what people call a chariot!"

"Stay down, Simeon. Yes, I think that's what it is, but there's more than one now. There must be a whole army of them!"

Swiftly the chariots approached.

The horses' feet beat quick rhythms as the whips sounded over their heads, and the drivers stood up behind them in the great iron chariots. The first passed close enough to fill the eyes of Deborah and Simeon with the dry dust of the road, and as they wiped away the grime, still another pounded by.

"It's gone, Deborah!" breathed Simeon.

But even as he spoke there was more rumbling and noise of iron wheels as a third chariot thundered down the road.

The boy and girl sat back in amazement. They had heard the men of their tribe talk of Egyptian and Canaanite chariots, but never before had they seen one so close to them. Never before had they been so frightened. Never before had they felt so alone.

Automatically they brushed the dirt from their tunics and rubbed at their faces with dusty hands. Then, fearfully they stood up.

Would there soon be another rumbling? Would other chariots soon descend upon them? And the next time, would they be discovered in their hiding place?

"Who were they, Deborah?"

"I don't know, Simeon."

"Well, I wonder where they were going."

"I don't know, Simeon. I just don't know. They were certainly not Hebrew people. Maybe they were Egyptians, like the men we saw in the marketplace of Bethel that day. Or they could have been Canaanites or even Philistines from over near the seacoast. There was so much dust, and I was so frightened, that I could not see the men clearly."

"Could they not have been from one of the other tribes of Israel, Deborah?"

"I don't think so. Our people know little of such means of travel. No, Simeon, they were not Hebrews, and iron chariots can only mean danger for Israel. If these people are *our* enemies, then they are enemies of the Lord, also."

"Maybe we should go back and tell Tirzah about this, Deborah," suggested Simeon fearfully.

Deborah shook her head slowly.

"Mother can do nothing about the chariots and we cannot either. Our job is to find Father. Only the men will know what to do. Father and Benjamin can tell us who would own such chariots. It's more important than ever that we find them now, Simeon."

Deborah stepped out into the road. Not even a distant

rumbling could be heard now, as the dust began to settle on the even tracks.

"Come, Simeon, let us go on, but let's not stay so close by the road this time."

The ground was uneven, and stones pushed up in hidden places bruised their toes and made walking very slow. Deborah's right leg and ankle throbbed from the unaccustomed exercise.

As they cut across a barren field and headed toward the hills before them, they felt safer and farther removed from the rumbling of the chariots. As confidence crept slowly back to the brother and sister, the sun grew hotter, and by noon hunger had almost replaced their fear.

Unwrapping a small bread loaf for each of them, Deborah offered Simeon some of the water from the skin they had brought from home.

"I wonder what Mother is doing now," mused Deborah, sitting on a large stone and rubbing her ankle slowly.

"I'd like to know where Father and Benjamin are," interrupted her impatient brother.

"We'll find them in those hills right ahead, Simeon. I'm just sure we will."

"Sure we will. Come on, then. If we're going to find them soon, we'd better keep going."

Deborah carefully put the other bread rolls back in the cloth package and picked up the waterskin. Stretching her arms, she thought how good it would be to lie down in the bushes and rest for just a little while. She knew her ankle would feel better, too, after a longer stop. With another quick gesture, however, she pulled back her shoulders and walked forward.

"The Lord goes with us in our search, Simeon. Come, now. We *will* not fail."

After walking for more than an hour, Simeon stopped a moment.

"How can a hill look so very near, and be so far away, Deborah?"

Deborah paused and looked about her. "It is a far distance," she agreed.

"I see no sign of flocks, Deborah."

"Nor I, Simeon, but we will soon. Come, let's go around to the right. There is a small path this way."

"But there's a path here to the left, also, Deborah. How do we know which way we should go?"

They stopped bewildered, but suddenly Deborah struck out for the path on her right. Simeon followed, too tired by now to argue about something neither seemed to have the slightest knowledge about.

"Look, Simeon, over past that ledge. I'm sure there will be a flat place and one good for sheep there. Father and Benjamin will surely be there!"

Simeon was now using the long staff in an effort to push himself forward, but it was doubtful whether the staff gave or required more energy for its use.

"See, Simeon, we can soon see past the ledge. How good it will be to see Father and Benjamin!"

Almost running in her eagerness, Deborah hurried toward the stony place that jutted out of the hill. Up she scrambled over the ledge. Her father and brother would surely be there!

Deborah turned, her face full of disappointment. Slumping to the ground, she buried her face in her arms as sobs shook her slim shoulders.

"Simeon, Simeon, it's all my fault! We went the way I said and now I'm wrong! What can we do now? How will we *ever* find Father?"

The young boy stooped down by his sister.

"Please, Deborah, don't cry now. I don't know the right direction either. I don't know which way we should go, but don't cry, Deborah. It just makes me feel worse. We'll surely think of something!"

Quieting her sobs, Deborah raised her face from her arms and wiped at the tears with her dusty hands. Stifling the last of her sighs, she stood up with determination and walked over to pick up a stick lying on the ground nearby.

"Here, I know how we will decide which way to go. I shall break this stick into a smaller and a larger piece, and one piece I will put into my right hand and one into my left hand. Both will be behind my back so you can't see them, Simeon, but you will choose which hand we shall follow.

"If you pick the hand with the shorter stick, we will go on from here, but if you pick the hand with the longer one, we will go back to the place where the two paths began. This will be a sign from God, Simeon. I have seen the men casting lots in ways like this, so we shall do it, too," Deborah broke the stick with a snapping motion, and held the uneven pieces behind her back.

Simeon knew that this was the way in which many problems of the tribe were decided, so he said with little hesitation, "Left hand."

Deborah held out the longer stick in her left hand.

"Let's start back," said the girl.

"All the way?" asked Simeon. "Can't we rest awhile?"

"No," Deborah answered firmly, though her leg ached and her whole body seemed to cry out for rest.

"It has been decided. Come, we must go back to the place where the paths separated. From there God will lead us on the other path that you first suggested, Simeon."

"But, please, Deborah, I'm *so* tired. Can't we stay here for tonight? We'll start back to the other path first thing tomorrow morning. Look, it's beginning to get dark already."

Deborah looked at the redness of the sky, for the sun had begun to set, and then she looked carefully at her brother. It was true, they were both very, very tired, from all the walking and all the experiences of the day. If only she were older and wiser, Deborah wished. But perhaps it would be better for them to sleep here in this small valley, and then look for the other path at dawn. Deborah wondered if this were her own best judgment speaking or just her tired body.

"We will stay here tonight, Simeon."

"Good, then let's eat. I'm hungry. And thirsty, too!"

Deborah shook the waterskin. There seemed plenty for some time, and surely they would find Father and Benjamin tomorrow. Carefully she handed the waterskin to Simeon.

With a more worried look, she unwrapped the bread loaves. Only three small loaves remained. She broke one in half and gave a piece to Simeon, who eagerly gobbled down the bread and would have reached for another had Deborah not shaken her head.

"But I'm still hungry, and we walked so far today. Can't we eat some more now? *Please,* Deborah!"

His sister broke another loaf in half and handed one piece to Simeon, but the other she put back in the cloth. Deborah was certain that Yahweh was leading them, but she was not quite certain how quickly.

"I wonder what Benjamin is doing now," mused Simeon, with the admiration he constantly held for his older brother.

"*I* wonder about Mother—if she is worried and if she is all right, too. Do you suppose the new baby will come while we are gone, Simeon?"

"I don't know much about babies, Deborah. When *do* they usually come?"

"I really don't know either, Simeon, but I do wish our family would be all in one place when the time does come."

"Maybe we will be," answered her brother eagerly.

"Yes. *Maybe,*" replied Deborah more slowly.

Chapter 5

"The paths come together not very far from here. I'm sure of it, Deborah," cried Simeon, running ahead in the early dawn.

"All right, but let's be sure to take the left course this time. We *must* find Father and Benjamin today."

At least, thought Deborah, it was a new day and it seemed to be a good one. Both she and her brother seemed to possess more enthusiasm and hope for the morning.

"Watch out, Simeon, be careful of that ledge!"

They edged themselves along a narrow place on the side of the hill.

"Look! Look up ahead!"

There *were* sheep ahead. They made a white pattern on the green carpet of the low, gently curving hillside.

Deborah could hardly contain herself.

"It's Father. I'm sure it is!" shouted Simeon.

Spurred by new hope, the brother and sister ran along the rough path, with Deborah's ankle slowing her but a very little.

"It *is* Father."

"I'm sure that's Benjamin's cloak."

"Deborah, come on!"

"Hurry, Simeon!"

And in the small valley, two of the shepherds looked to the hillside.

"Benjamin, is that not Simeon and Deborah running toward us?" cried Zelophad.

"It is indeed!" shouted Benjamin, starting to run in the direction of his younger brother and sister.

What a joyous meeting!

Zelophad put his arms warmly about his younger son and Benjamin lifted Deborah off from the ground in a great bear-like embrace.

"Yahweh be praised! But why are you here? Has anything happened at the tents?" questioned Zelophad.

"And Mother, has anything happened to her? Is she all right? Why have you come and how did you find us?" questioned Benjamin.

"Why have you not come home?" broke in Simeon.

"It is you whom we have been worried about," persisted Deborah.

"Let us all sit down and talk one at a time," suggested Zelophad.

"There is a well here in this valley and you can get water here. But rest now, and listen to those things that have happened. But first, my children, what about your mother? How is she now?" Zelophad asked again in a worried tone.

Deborah thought about her mother wearily carrying the water jugs, but she looked also at the anxiety on the face of her father.

"Mother is well. It was she who sent us to look for you. We have been so afraid for you."

"We were on our way home three days ago when a small band of Canaanites came against us in the fields and killed many of the sheep and goats. Two Canaanite men were killed and your mother's brother Ishmael died, too. They came upon us while we were tending the sheep and they demanded that we leave this land forever."

"And then," interrupted Benjamin, "we heard that a whole army of Canaanites were ready to march against us in that very place if we did not leave immediately."

"We thought it best not to return immediately, lest we lead the Canaanite soldiers to the tents. Jepthah, our cousin, knew of this valley, so we brought the sheep here."

"Perhaps," added Benjamin, "we can all go back to the tents tomorrow. Then we must move the tribe further south."

"I fear for Mother to travel far just now," said Deborah with concern.

"We must all travel together. Only by our families staying close to one another is there any hope of safety. Mother will go with us." Zelophad was firm in his statement of the decision.

"But how did you ever find us?" asked Benjamin.

"It was Deborah and the Lord and some sticks," Simeon said, as he told them about the drawing of the lots.

"But, Father, there was something else which terrified us yesterday," said Deborah. "As we walked along the road three iron chariots sped past us. Were these the Canaanites who attacked you?"

"No, Deborah, I do not think so. It is true that the Canaanites do have many chariots of iron, but so also do the Philistines and the Egyptians. Others, too, are known to have such implements of travel. The Canaanites who attacked us were on horseback, and fewer than a dozen in number."

The four, anxious in heart for the future but joyful in their reunion, sat quietly for a few moments with one another. The sheep grazed contentedly and the few goats among them bleated without annoyance.

"Look, Simeon, look at the lamb in the bushes. Here, take my staff so that it won't become more tangled in the thorns."

Simeon jumped up with an expression of pure delight on his face.

Deborah and Benjamin looked at one another with smiles of happiness and understanding. They both knew how proud Simeon was to carry his father's staff, and it was indeed a sign of praise not often given to a boy so young.

Proudly Simeon carried the staff and tenderly he loosed the lamb from the briars, picking the thorns from the soft fleece with his hands.

"Look, Benjamin, who is that on the other hill?" Deborah asked, laying her hand on her older brother's arm.

"It looks like the Canaanites again," whispered Benjamin.

Zelophad had already stood up and was motioning toward the other shepherds.

When the men had gathered, Zelophad said, "Now is the time; let us go up and talk with them."

"Very well," answered the older Jepthah. "We will make a sign to them of our peaceful intent."

Saying this, he moved toward the edge of the valley in the direction of the men. His right arm he raised above his head as in blessing.

Zelophad hesitated and then turned toward his children.

"Simeon and Deborah, you must stay here. Benjamin, you take them to the cave behind the bushes. Stay there quietly. Make no sudden motions lest they suspect we are hiding other men to fight against them. We will go now to talk to the Canaanites, but remember, stay close to Benjamin."

Briskly Zelophad moved off to join Jepthah and the other men.

"Come on. Follow me," cried Benjamin. And he herded Deborah and Simeon toward the cave that was now visible behind the bushes where the lamb had been caught.

"Those Canaanites, I despise them!" muttered Benjamin as he spat upon the floor of the cave.

"Well, why don't we fight them, if we hate them so much?" asked Simeon.

"It's quite simple, young brother. If there was a war, they would be sure to win it. The Canaanites have many many swords and spears and all kinds of fighting implements. It is these things which count on a battle line. How can you fight with a wooden shepherd's staff?"

Simeon had grown brave and daring from his trip with Deborah and from the honor of carrying Zelophad's favorite staff.

"I could do something. I know I could. I'm sure Father needs me up there with the men. I'm a man now. I have been brave these past two days and I can be brave again."

"Hush, Simeon," quieted Deborah. "Father knows what is best for us. Just stay here and be quiet."

"I can't stand it not doing anything. I know I could help if I only could hear what Father and the other men are saying. You've always told me I was too young, but Father knows I'm not. I'm *going* to help . . ."

Before Benjamin or Deborah could lay a hand on his shoulder Simeon had darted past them and out into the clearing. As he pushed from behind the bushes, a Canaanite soldier thought his motion signaled the beginning of a surprise attack, and with but a single movement, the Canaanite hurled a spear in the direction from which Simeon had burst.

There was so little noise.

For Deborah there was only terror.

Swiftly she and Benjamin dashed to the place where Simeon had fallen. The boy lay motionless before the bushes. The spear, that with its swiftness and weight of its thrust had hit the side of his head, now lay buried several feet beyond his body.

"Simeon!" cried Deborah.

Benjamin knelt quickly by his brother, and lifted his limp body into his strong arms.

"Is he breathing, Benjamin?"

"I don't know, Deborah, I don't know."

"Simeon, open your eyes! Simeon, look at us!"

But the eyelids did not flutter and the mouth did not move.

Zelophad had reached the place now. Swiftly he laid his son upon the ground, placed his ear to his chest, and warily lifted the limp eyelids.

Suddenly sobs wracked the body of Zelophad. He turned from the boy and began beating his arms upon his chest.

"My son is dead!" he cried. "Simeon my beloved son has been killed!"

Deborah looked with horror at Benjamin. Surely it could not be true!

And then suddenly her breath drew in sharply as she stooped and picked up the leather strap so beloved by Simeon which had come loose from the belt at his waist when he fell.

"Look, Benjamin, this is all we have left that was Simeon's," Deborah sobbed. "And it was those Canaanites, those enemies of our people, who killed Simeon!"

Angrily Benjamin shook his fist at the hillside, but already the Canaanites had disappeared.

Deborah buried her face in her hands.

"I *will* do something about this. Now I am too young, as Simeon was too young, but someday it will be different. When I am grown, we Hebrews will know revenge. I vow, by Almighty Yahweh, this day, that the Canaanites will not be forgiven and that they will feel the anger and wrath of my family and my people!"

Zelophad said nothing, but knelt weeping loudly above the body of his son.

"Sackcloth and ashes must be brought to me," he wailed. "Sackcloth and ashes I must put on that I may weep in pain and in anguish for this my son."

Benjamin and the other men of the tribe moved almost helplessly about. Finally, with reluctance, Benjamin stooped down and picked up a large stone. There were many stones to be picked up now, for the grave of Simeon must be well marked, that all Israelites might one day know of the boy who had tried so eagerly to help his people, and who had died with so few years of his life having been spent.

Clutching the leather strap tightly in her hand, Deborah looked at each stone the men placed for the grave marking. She would not forget a single stone, she promised herself. This gentle boy, who wanted most in the world to make beautiful things with his hands—dead. This strap in her hand and these stones of his grave she would remember forever.

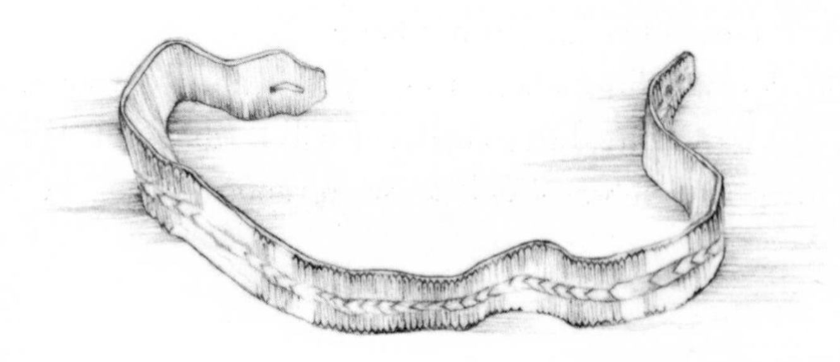

Chapter 6

It was three years now since Simeon had been killed. The tribes of Manasseh and Naphtali, as well as Ephraim, still had frequent trouble from the Canaanites. Other Israelite tribes of Dan and Judah told of battles with the Philistines and the Sea People. In spite of all these discouragements, the Hebrews continued their sheepherding and goat-raising. Yahweh had promised them this land, and he would keep his promise, they assured one another.

The baby, Huldah, who had been born to Tirzah the very day after Simeon's death, now was a jolly romping child who trotted affectionately after her big sister, Deborah.

Zelophad and the other families of their tribe had moved frequently, constantly seeking better lands for grazing, and hoping to avoid property battles with the Canaanites, who continually became more infuriated at the presence of the Hebrew people anywhere in the land.

Benjamin was now almost as tall as his father, and it was rumored that Zelophad was making arrangements for Benjamin to marry his third cousin, Miriam, a tall, slim girl, the daughter of Asahiah. Deborah had always admired Miriam's sleek, black hair and her way of getting what she wished merely by the raising of her shoulders, the tossing of her head, or the shedding of a few loud tears.

Benjamin was obviously well pleased with the proposed marriage. Eagerly he confided to Deborah that Zelophad had been forced to offer Asahiah three goats and five sheep in payment for this black-haired daughter.

Miriam had known Benjamin all her life. It was not only that their tents had never been far from one another, but they were of the same large family and of the same tribe of Israel. It mattered little to Miriam that soon she would be under the patriarchal rule of Zelophad, since she, as a woman, was marrying into the family of her husband.

Asahiah, her father, had always been stern in the discipline of his household and shrewd in the management of his flocks. Asahiah demanded now that Zelophad add a final fifth lamb to the payment, and Miriam was secretly pleased that Zelophad had accepted her father's demand. As for Benjamin, her husband-to-be, Miriam was delighted that he was one of the most trusted young men of their tribe, as well as one of the most handsome. How proud she was that a man so good-looking and so strong of arm was to be acquired as her husband!

The time was set for the marriage feast. Deborah could sense the excitement in the air. She hoped she would be a good sister-in-law to Miriam. She admired the girl's assurance and

her beauty. Pushing back a wisp of her own unruly hair, Deborah wondered if perhaps she didn't envy Miriam for other reasons also.

What abilities did Miriam possess that would make Zelophad, her usually cautious father, pay the extra sheep that Asahiah demanded in order to gain Miriam as a daughter-in-law? Benjamin, too, seemed more joyful in the last few days and occasionally let a whistle escape from his lips as he let the sheep out of the fold each morning or placed his shepherd's staff by a tent corner each evening.

Tirzah was now adding extra epahs of flour for the baking of the bread for the wedding feast and for the extra honey cakes so greatly anticipated by all the tribe. Deborah was busy, too, rearranging the clay lamp and the goatskin jugs and all the equipment of their family life, for Miriam would be moving into the tent now, as a new member of the household of Zelophad, and room must be made for the new daughter-in-law.

A thought possessed Deborah as the wedding time drew near. What about her? The head of what family in their tribe would be willing to buy her for his son? Would she ever be so desired as the beautiful Miriam? Suppose no one *ever* wanted her?

The time of the wedding finally arrived. Early in the morning Asahiah led Miriam, heavily veiled, with clothes woven new for the occasion, to the place he and Zelophad had decided to meet. Zelophad and Miriam were followed by a joyous and singing procession of bridesmaids and kinspeople.

Deborah sang the old songs of happiness and well-wishing, too, as she followed her father and Benjamin as they went to join Zelophad and Miriam. Deborah looked at Benjamin proudly. He stood tall and straight, and looked so handsome in his rich new wedding cloak.

Zelophad greeted the bridal party. "The feast is prepared," he said, "come to my tent." As was the custom, the feasting would last for seven days, and there would be much singing and dancing. A wedding was a happy time for all.

Lambs had been killed for the feast, and there was more roast lamb and goat's milk than Deborah could remember having seen in one place for a long time. There were figs and dates, too, and small cakes made by Tirzah from the precious honey they saved for very special occasions.

After all had eaten their fill, Asahiah rose to his feet, with Miriam close behind him. Zelophad and Benjamin rose now, too, and a hush fell over the feasting people.

"Zelophad," said Asahiah, "I bring you Miriam, my daughter, to be wife to your son, Benjamin."

The two fathers stood aside and spoke a few words to each other that Deborah could not hear. Deborah wondered if Asahiah had decided at the last moment to ask for another goat. But all was well, for now Benjamin stepped up to Miriam and spread his cloak around her shoulders. Then they turned from the crowd and went inside the tent of Zelophad where a special bridal chamber had been prepared for them.

The feasting continued. Amid the singing and the loud

merrymaking, Deborah reflected on her happiness for Benjamin and Miriam. She was glad that Benjamin had not, as some Israelites had done, taken a Canaanite or Amorite or Moabite wife. Such marriages displeased Yahweh, because these foreign women brought their many gods with them.

When the feasting began to wane, people settled in their family groups and chanted songs with one another. As always, their favorite entertainment was the telling of stories. Always these were stories of the people of Israel—stories of their victories and their accomplishments, stories of their battles, their love for one another, stories of their obedience and their disastrous disobedience of the Almighty Lord.

Deborah could hear her Uncle Caleb in one corner of the group reciting the story of Abraham's search for a wife for his son, Isaac. Deborah was too far back in the crowd to see her uncle, but she knew how vigorously he would be shaking his fist to emphasize the historical command of Abraham to his servant, "And I will make thee swear by the LORD, the God of heaven, and the God of the earth, that thou shalt *not* take a wife unto my son of the daughters of the Canaanites among whom I dwell: but thou shalt go unto *my* country, and to *my* kindred, and take a wife unto my son Isaac."

Deborah smiled. Isaac had married the beautiful Rebekah, who was indeed one of their own people, since Rebekah's grandfather had been a brother of Abraham, father of all the Hebrew people. One day she hoped that she, too, would marry a man of her own people, just as Rebekah many years before and now Miriam had done. This was a thought Deborah had often.

From another corner of the crowd came the sound of music and the delicate playing of the flute. Deborah wandered in the direction of the sound, and she saw Lapidoth, the brother of Miriam. He was sitting on the ground, earnestly playing as if to himself.

"Play on," urged one of the men nearby, as the musician paused for a moment.

"Tell us a story, Lapidoth," encouraged another.

"You play well, young man, but it is your storytelling that makes my heart glad," said another of the old shepherds, whose shoulders were bent from many years of walking over the hills of Canaan but whose eyes were bright and glistening from the excitement of the wedding holiday.

Deborah had known Lapidoth, just as she had known Miriam, all her life. They were part of the same tribe, the intermingling of families that together sheep-herded and feasted and worshiped Yahweh as true Hebrew people. Last autumn all their families had together made the journey to Shechem to sacrifice to Yahweh in his own tabernacle and to pray by the holy of holies, the Ark of the Covenant, that their people had guarded and cherished so zealously since the days of their wanderings. On that particular trip, Deborah's eyes had met those of Lapidoth on several occasions, and for both of them there had been brief smiles and a dropping of their heads.

It was now with more than casual interest that Deborah

stopped to listen to familiar tones and inflections. The voice of Lapidoth seemed to blend with the sounds of the crowd, and yet it sounded distinct and as musical as the flute he had played a few moments before.

"And this is the story of Jacob," began Lapidoth, as the women settled themselves upon the ground and the men drew close to the boy who had so early learned the stories of their ancestors.

"For Jacob was the son of Isaac who was the son of Abraham . . ."

Deborah half smiled, for all the stories began with the recitation of the hero's ancestors. So few things could be written down, but family histories were remembered for centuries by the constant repetition of the story at every feast and at every gathering together of the tribes. All of these stories were dear to Deborah.

"And Jacob dearly loved the younger daughter of Laban, the well-favored Rachel. So well did he love Rachel that for seven years he served Laban that he might earn this younger daughter as his wife . . ."

Deborah sighed. This was the favorite story of all wedding feasts. Surely no one would ever love her as dearly as Jacob had loved Rachel.

Quickly Deborah brought her own eyes back to the thin face of Lapidoth.

The storytelling had made him overcome his shyness, and his enthusiasm for the telling made his face intensely alive. His dark eyes burned with the fervor of his emotion as he told of the disappointment of Jacob upon receiving Laban's older daughter as his wife, after having worked for seven years for the hand of Rachel.

"So dearly, however, did Jacob love Rachel," continued Lapidoth, "that for seven more years did he work that he might finally have Rachel as his wife."

Deborah walked slowly back to the tent, and went inside thoughtfully to lay down upon her straw mat. How strong and handsome the thin Lapidoth seemed when he was caught up in the storytelling. What was it that made this man seem so handsome and so attractive?

It must be, reasoned Deborah, the quiet persuasiveness of his voice and the deep burning of his dark eyes, or maybe, just maybe, it was only the wonderful stories themselves. But of this, Deborah was not very certain.

Thinking about the feast outside, Deborah heard a noise behind the curtains in the main section of the tent. Immediately, as a man spoke, Deborah recognized the voice of Zelophad, her father.

"It is good, my cousin, that our families are again united. Miriam is a strong girl and she can work both in the tent and the fields for Benjamin. Surely, too, she will bear him many sons."

Deborah knew then that it was Asahiah who had joined Zelophad on the other side of the curtain from where she lay quietly on the mat.

"Your Benjamin is a good son," Asahiah said slowly, almost weighing each word, "and I am glad Miriam will be a part of your household. Now, however, I have another matter that I come to discuss with you."

"And what is that, my good cousin Asahiah?"

"It is my son, Lapidoth. He was given that name, meaning "firebrand," for I had dreams that he would become the greatest fighter in the tribe and the strongest defender of all our families. How disappointing it is that the defending of the tribe and the fighting of our battles has such little interest for him. It seems only in the telling of stories, on such a day as this, that I can see any of the "fire" in his eyes or burning from his heart."

Zelophad did not answer.

A man did not condemn the son of another unless he had real cause. Zelophad had never thought of Lapidoth as the most promising young man of their tribe, but he kept the laws of Yahweh.

Deborah held her breath to hear her father's reply, but none came.

Asahiah paid little attention to the silence.

"I have come to bargain with you, son of Abraham. I would buy from you the elder of your daughters, the dreamy-eyed Deborah, as a wife for Lapidoth. Surely since both of them have their eyes on faraway clouds and hills, they would make a fine match for each other."

Asahiah laughed, but there was little merriment in the sound.

Deborah lay huddled on her straw mat, hardly daring to

breathe lest her presence be discovered. She and Lapidoth. She had scarcely dreamed of such a possibility. Should she be glad or dismayed? At the moment, she was only fearful of discovery.

"Perhaps it can be done, Asahiah. Perhaps it can be done," answered Zelophad.

It had been with much reluctance that Zelophad had parted with three goats and five sheep to secure Miriam for Benjamin, and now here was his same kinsman offering him a chance to gain back the missing part of his flock.

"Perhaps it *can* be done, Asahiah. Perhaps it can be done," repeated Zelophad with more assurance.

"Zelophad," began Asahiah in his most cordial manner, while Deborah strained to catch every word and inflection of his voice, "your daughter is a fine young Hebrew woman, yet you must admit that she is not so fair to look upon as your new daughter-in-law, Miriam. Too, she is older than most of our women when they are betrothed. Miriam has known only thirteen summers, but Deborah has known fifteen."

Behind the curtain, Deborah could feel her breath draw in and her heart begin to pound loudly.

"Deborah is quick about her work," Asahiah continued, "but there is a frailness about her. Her leg is weak, surely that is why no one has asked for her before now. I do not think she will be of much help in the bearing of my family's work. For her, I can give you only two sheep."

"Two sheep!" Deborah heard her Father laugh. "Asahiah,

my cousin, you are indeed jesting! Never have you seen a woman more able than Deborah, nor a girl more sure-footed on the hill paths when sheep have strayed away. Not for eight sheep would I give up such a daughter. No! No, indeed! Not for eight sheep and six goats could I give up such a woman to become the wife of Lapidoth!"

Deborah now sat up angrily, her fury rising steadily against the burly Asahiah. Two sheep! Why, this was nothing for the payment for a wife! Surely her father would not sell her for such a price! How could Asahiah dare to bargain for her so low! Deborah's pride was crushed as her anger mounted!

But Zelophad knew well the crafty Asahiah, and he was well acquainted with the "man talk" connected with the buying and selling of daughters. He objected little to the implication that Deborah was weak and less than beautiful. He himself had cast remarks to Asahiah only weeks before as to the lack of diligence and industry of Miriam, in order that he might pay less on the marriage day.

Deborah, however, had never heard such conversations, and she imagined herself as the only girl thus haggled about. Her fists clenched and her eyes burned with fury against the red-haired kinsman!

"Well, perhaps one goat along with the two sheep," Asahiah conceded.

"One goat, you say!" argued Zelophad his arms crossed on his wide chest.

"One goat and only two sheep! You are out of your mind,

Asahiah. Only because you are my kinsman will I give Deborah to you for seven sheep and four goats, but, remember, they must be healthy milk-giving creatures."

"Oh, son of Abraham, you know well that all the flocks of Asahiah are of the strongest stock and the pride of all our people," countered the bargainer.

"But to show how much I respect the family of Zelophad, I will add another goat to my price. But no more. This is all I shall pay for that weak, dreaming daughter of yours!"

"Now, Asahiah . . ."

But, at that moment the flap of the tent was pulled open and in burst the toddling Huldah, wailing loudly, "Deb'rah, Deb'rah! I want my sister!"

Seeing little reaction to her tears, Huldah stamped her small feet upon the dirt floor, pounded her brown fists in the air, and bellowed, "Deb'rah! Deb'rah! I want Deb'rah!"

Then with the directness of a spear, Huldah darted for the women's section of the tent. Swiftly she grabbed back the curtain.

"Deb'rah!"

And Deborah stood, disregarding Huldah, her face flushed with fury and her eyes burning with anger at this "bargainer-for-her-life," the would-be father-in-law, Asahiah.

Zelophad looked at his daughter in amazement. How long could his daughter have been behind those curtains? He was annoyed at her presence. Women seemed to be in all the places where they were not wanted.

Asahiah looked at the girl, lifted one eyebrow, then put his hands on his hips, threw back his head and laughed loudly.

With the laughter of sarcasm still in his voice, he reached out and putting his hand on the shoulder of Deborah said with a loud guffaw, "Ah, good! The wife for Lapidoth is a pretty one when angry! Maybe that anger will kindle some spark in that "firebrand" son of mine. Maybe it will burn him to be more than a mere "singer of songs"!

Fury still flashing in her eyes, Deborah pulled herself away from Asahiah's hand and, holding her head erect with her voice constrained, she announced coldly: "Gladly will I become the wife of Lapidoth. Obediently will I serve your family, Asahiah. But never, and this I swear unto you this day, never, stern father of Lapidoth, will you see the son that I shall one day bear for Lapidoth!"

With no further word, Deborah disappeared into the night away from the tent of her father. Her anger at Asahiah was so intense that she was almost frightened by her own feelings. And the words she had hurled in fury at her kinsman—she realized now—she ought never to have said. Why had she said them? Surely such a dread prophecy would never come true!

In the darkness, Deborah knew that her marriage to Lapidoth had been arranged, but she wished she could be as certain that her words hurled out in anger and hurt pride would never come to pass.

Chapter 7

In the weeks that followed, Deborah knew that the marriage had been arranged and that the wedding time was quickly approaching, although the arrangements were not hers and the plans were not those of Lapidoth. She saw the thin young man no more often now than in previous months, and always, if she happened to encounter him near the tent or down by the well, their eyes would drop down with embarrassment.

From the instant of Asahiah's bargaining, she had devoted herself to "discovering" Lapidoth. Although she dropped her eyes and turned away at his approach, Deborah, in her instinctive girl-fashion, was listening intensely and watching avidly.

Her ears were now always alert to the sound of his voice, and the natural rhythm of his speaking seemed in her heart. Evenings, she found her feet walking deliberately near the tent of Asahiah on the pretext of exercise. Her heart pounded delightedly when she heard the low tones of his voice.

Miriam watched with lifted eyebrows, for she had already been married four months.

"Deborah, that brother of mine isn't worth all that attention!" she commented in a mocking voice when her sister-in-law returned from an evening walk.

Deborah regarded Miriam with puzzlement. She had looked forward to having a sister near her own age, for the child Huldah was like a baby and Deborah had known only brothers in her growing-up years.

She had imagined it would be fun sharing secrets with Miriam, planning her marriage with Benjamin's wife to help. Miriam, however, was little interested in Deborah's plans. Lying on the mat and running a comb through her sleek black hair, she remarked in a matter-of-fact tone, "Of course, Lapidoth isn't doing so well for himself either. Imagine getting a wife with a twisted foot!"

With this parting barb, Miriam rose and disappeared behind the curtain of the inner tent.

With hurt and astonishment, Deborah looked at her foot!

It was true she could not move it as easily since her fall three years ago, but she had never before thought of her leg as twisted. Her foot might seem a little crooked, perhaps, but surely not twisted!

Is this what Lapidoth thought also? Was he really ashamed to marry her! Did *he* think he was getting only a bride with a twisted foot?

Suddenly she knew what she would do—what she must do! She'd ask him—and ask him now! Even the promises of her father to Asahiah would never make her go through such a marriage if Lapidoth thought of her with pity—as a cripple!

She sped from the tent toward the familiar one of Asahiah. See, she *could* run, she assured herself! Maybe not so gracefully as Miriam, but she could tend sheep and bake bread more expertly than Benjamin's wife who had little interest in anything that did not beautify her or add to her leisure time.

But what did *Lapidoth* think of her? That's what she really wanted to know! That's what really mattered!

At the tent door she paused. It was evening and darkness had fallen, but she could see the shadows from the oil lamp reflecting the family of Asahiah within the tent. She had no desire to talk with the abrupt Asahiah nor listen to his barked orders about sons' and daughters' duties to their parents! But how to attract Lapidoth's attention?

She tossed a few small stones at the doorpost of the tent and in a few moments saw a figure move towards the opening. Deborah drew a sigh of relief. The shadow was certainly not large enough for the burly Asahiah.

How surprised she was when the door-skin was pulled back and Deborah saw the bent figure of Sarah, the grandmother of Lapidoth.

Deborah held her fingers to her lips in a gesture of silence, and the old woman nodded and smiled as she let the tent door fall behind her.

Together the old and the young woman walked a few yards from the tent in the mild summer evening.

"How could your ears have heard those pebbles I threw?"

The old woman winked and shook a finger in Deborah's face.

"Perhaps it was not my ears that heard, Deborah, but my heart! Now, why come you at this time to the tent of Asahiah? What brings you out now?"

"I cannot marry Lapidoth. I cannot. I just cannot, Grandmother Sarah!"

The bright eyes peered out from the wrinkled face.

"Hush now, young Deborah. How strange you talk! Not marry the fine straight Lapidoth, my own dearest grandson! Why do you speak such nonsense?"

The sharp notes of indignation softened, however, as she saw Deborah's troubled face.

"What bothers you, little one?" she asked more quietly now, putting her frail arm about the waist of the tall girl.

With a burst of feeling Deborah let the words tumble out as they would.

"That's it . . . just what you said, Grandmother Sarah . . . you are right. Lapidoth is fine and straight and tall . . . he's too fine and too straight to have me, with my twisted leg, as his wife!"

"Do you have a twisted leg, Deborah? I hadn't noticed. I have only seen your eyes shine with compassion, and your heart hold kindness, while your hands worked willingly for those who could not help themselves. I never noticed your foot, Deborah, and Lapidoth will not see it either. If you build for him a tent of love, he will see only your devotion."

Deborah looked almost dazed at the old woman. Could the grandmother be right? But it was such a long, long time since she had been young!

"And now, off with you, Deborah! Back to your own tent! It's much too late for an unmarried girl to be out roaming about the tents. Off with you now and be busy with the wedding plans! How can you please Lapidoth if you have not stitched your wedding veils well?"

Back to her own tent hobbled the grandmother, and back to the tent of her father scurried Deborah.

As she drifted to sleep on her straw mat that night, she began to wonder just how many more rows of embroidery she should put on her veils. Where would be the best place to find the herbs for the bright dyes? Grandmother Sarah was right, Deborah decided. She *had* to be right!

But while Deborah's mind was filled with plans for the wedding day, the men of the tribe were meeting in deep plans and utter seriousness. Must they move the whole tribe? Nearer and nearer and more frequent had come the attacks by the Canaanites in the last months.

Some of the families of Ephraim had already moved east of the Jordan River in the past weeks. Could all of them go south towards Egypt now or West nearer the sea?

All of them knew that enemies of the Hebrews lived in these places, also. The People of the Sea violently attacked the tribes by the seacoast and the Egyptian power would crush their people or bind them into slavery again if they moved southward.

They could not move, and yet daily tales of Canaanite harassment and murders reached their ears. The main highways of the land were not safe for any lone travelers, and Canaanite atrocities seemed to be committed more frequently each month.

Life in the tribe of Ephraim seemed more unsettled than the men had known in many years.

As the women prepared for the marriage of Deborah, the men prepared for sudden and uncertain attack by the Canaanites. Men took turns at the watch from the highest point around their tents, and even though the plans were made and carried out by the men alone, the women sensed an uneasiness in the air. Both Tirzah and Deborah felt a restlessness not brought on by the mere preparation for the wedding.

"Nothing will happen now," Tirzah assured her daughter. "First will come your beautiful and happy wedding, and only after that will we think of the fighting and our enemies."

But a mother's love sometimes makes her hopes more strong for peace than is her knowledge for the facts of war.

Grandmother Sarah had been delightedly busy, making up cakes with a rich date filling.

"This recipe," she avowed "has been handed down among our people from generation to generation since Isaac married the beautiful Rebekah. It is even more fitting now that these cakes should be made again when the handsome Lapidoth, "firebrand" of the tribe takes unto himself the lovely Deborah!"

No, no one else but she herself could make these cakes! No one else was capable of such great care for the kneading of the dough. No, no one but she herself could possibly make this recipe!

When Deborah heard how Sarah was allowing nothing to be done for the feast without her own personal guidance, she smiled happily. How she loved old Sarah for all her obstinancy!

Sarah was the mother of Asahiah, but she had managed his household with a firm and forceful hand since his wife, the mother of Lapidoth and Miriam, had died some eight years before when an epidemic fever had spread across their tribe. Asahiah had always seemed too busy acquiring greater flocks to marry again. Sarah did not mind. She liked the running of households and people. It was satisfying to know she was needed in her old age.

Asahiah had now led the sheep and goats to the flocks of Zelophad and the wedding exchange was soon to be made.

Deborah awoke on her wedding morning and saw before her mat the striped shawl of red and gold that she had seen Grandmother Sarah working on for several months now. Sarah had always insisted that the bright scarf was for herself—to cheer her up on dark and dreary days. Deborah held it close to her face. What a beautiful, beautiful gift from the old woman who scolded the whole tribe so infuriatingly!

Deborah arose, and after the bridesmaids had helped her with the ceremonial bath, they carefully helped her dress and wrapped the veils about her face. No man must see her as she was led to the tent of Asahiah and the home of her new husband.

Zelophad stood waiting almost sternly, with his cloak brushed and manner unmoving. He was ready to lead his daughter away from the tent of their family for the last time. As Deborah approached her father, she could see, even through the veils, that Tirzah was blinking away the tears as she pretended to make herself busy with other tasks.

Benjamin came forward before she reached the door, and placing his arms roughly about her shoulders said softly, "Farewell, dear sister, I shall miss you deeply."

Deborah could see Miriam sitting in the corner with an expression of wistfulness upon her face.

The day is beautiful, thought Deborah, the most beautiful day in the world, the most beautiful day of all! Deborah's heart was so full of her happiness that she didn't notice the anxious looks the men cast among themselves, nor the fact that though they joined in the songs of well-wishing, their eyes were constantly watching the hills surrounding the camp.

Slowly, carefully keeping close behind Zelophad, Deborah walked to meet Asahiah and Lapidoth. Grandmother Sarah stood at the front of the bridegroom's party with her arms held out in a gesture of affection for her new granddaughter. Behind Sarah, Deborah could see Asahiah, and with him, her beloved Lapidoth.

The feasting began, and the time came when Deborah heard her father say, "Asahiah, I bring you Deborah to be wife to your son, Lapidoth." As if in a dream, Deborah felt Lapidoth place his cloak around her shoulders and gently lead her by the hand into the tent.

Gently Lapidoth began to pull away the veil from her face. With great tenderness, he seemed to be looking for the first time at the tall Deborah whom he had known all his life.

As their eyes met, they silently pledged their loyalty and love to each other.

Suddenly there was a roar that grew rapidly louder and a woman's shriek. There was a shout from the Hebrew guards of the tribe and the yelling of the men. Screams sounded through the tribe.

"The Canaanites!"

"The Canaanites are coming!"

"We are being attacked! Men, up and fight our enemies! Fight against the enemies of the Lord!"

Longingly Lapidoth drew his bride to him, then quickly stood upright and drew away from Deborah.

"I will return, beloved Deborah. I shall come back, and soon."

And suddenly, unbelievably on her wedding day, the time of the most joyous of all holidays—the wedding feast—Deborah was alone, alone in the tent of her husband, alone in the tent of Asahiah. Alone.

Deborah pulled back the tent flap. There was Grandmother Sarah some fifty yards away, shaking her fist angrily at the gathering dust of the horses.

Clad in her wedding robes, Deborah ran to Sarah and tried to lead the old woman back to her tent.

"No. I will have none of it. I shall not hide now. If I am to die, I will look at the swords of those Canaanite assassins. I will see the spear of those murderers. Never will I hide while those enemies of Yahweh ride their horses!"

The Canaanites were indeed riding their horses and straight for the tents of Ephraim. There seemed to be but a dozen soldiers in the attack, but each horseman carried in his hand a spear and each had a sword hung at his waist. All carried the implements of war, all except one, and he, in the lead, held a torch of flaming wood.

Deborah tried to pull the grandmother from the scene of terror, but Sarah wrenched herself free.

Onward the Canaanites came and each man broke out of line, scattering among the tents of Ephraim, and casting spears and arrows and swords at the Hebrew men, many of whom stood up to fight armed only with their shepherd staffs.

There seemed little direction in the plan of the Canaanite attack, except for the leader who rode straight, it seemed to Deborah, towards the tent of Asahiah.

In an instant, he had hurled his flaming torch at the very center post of the slanted roof. In an instant flames had enveloped the tent, for the hot dry heat of the summer day seemed to fan the destructive fire.

Sarah and Deborah looked unbelievingly at the flames!

Could this be their home, this flaming piece of rubble? Could this be the possessions of Sarah and Asahiah and Lapidoth, all becoming a hopeless mass of ashes before their eyes!

Terror now struck throughout the tribe. Women stood in panic before their tents clutching their children or huddled beside bushes lest they be seen by the Canaanites who now already seemed to be speeding away.

Men and women were trying to beat out the flames from the tent of Asahiah lest the fire spread through all of the tents. Women hastily drew water from the well and carried it in their jugs to throw upon the flames.

Asahiah screamed orders to the men and some climbed on donkeys to ride off in sluggish, awkward pursuit of the enemies. Many others, like Zelophad, were too bewildered to give aid in any direction. Most followed the dusty trail on foot.

Deborah had seen Lapidoth grab his staff and head towards the Canaanites when she first came out of the tent. Now, seeing Miriam standing close beside her with fright and panic in her eyes, Deborah knew that Benjamin, too, must have been among the early ones to give battle to the Canaanites.

Deborah looked with bewilderment at her sister-in-law whose white cheeks and quivering lips gave indication of her terror.

"We're all alone now, Deborah," she sobbed. "They've all gone away."

"No. We are not alone, Miriam. Yahweh the Lord is with us. And Benjamin and Lapidoth will soon return. Come, let us all go to Tirzah's tent."

"Come, Grandmother Sarah, you must come with us. The tent of Asahiah your son has been destroyed and you must now come with me," Deborah said firmly leading Sarah, who for the first time in her life, responded in a docile manner.

Miriam followed, too, but continued her hysterical sobbing. "I'll never see my husband again! Benjamin will die! I know he will never be back!"

"Hush, Miriam. You will only frighten Tirzah and Huldah more by such talk!"

Sarah, completely stunned by the tragedy of the past hour, seemed more composed than Miriam. Deborah led the grandmother to the tent of her parents, and the sympathetic Tirzah rushed forward to embrace the stooped figure and to give her the comfort she would need in the hours to come.

Miriam seemed beyond comfort or reasoning.

"I'm alone, Deborah! I'm all alone! Benjamin has gone off and left me here alone to be killed!"

"Benjamin will be back soon. He has gone to protect you, to save you, and all of us, from the Canaanites. The Canaanites must be destroyed if our people are to live. Benjamin fights for you and for all the tribe of Ephraim!"

"But what good will it do if he is killed? It is no good then," cried Miriam her body again shaking with her sobbing.

"Benjamin will be back, Miriam, but even if he were to die for our people, it would be worthwhile. He fights for the Lord God and for His people, Israel. Surely this is of worth to you."

"But I'm alone, Deborah. I'm all alone here."

"And I am alone, too. Have you forgotten that this is my wedding day—the most wonderful day of my life. We were to celebrate the marriage feast, and eat of the lamb and honey cakes and sing the songs of joy and happiness!"

Slowly, as Deborah spoke, Miriam ceased her weeping, and with swollen cheeks and red eyes looked with amazement at her sister-in-law.

"I had forgotten, Deborah. I had forgotten all about your wedding day! It is terrible then for you, too. It's terrible for you as well as for me! I'm sorry for you, Deborah. I'm terribly sorry, but I'm sorry for myself, also."

And again Miriam took up her sobbing.

"Yes, Miriam, it is terrible for me, too, but rather would I have Lapidoth die on our wedding day than have our tribe destroyed. The Canaanites are our enemies, and the enemies of the Lord, when they attack our people. Are you not proud that Benjamin goes to fight for his people?"

Miriam did not answer.

"Come now, then, let us go in and comfort Sarah. It is she who has lost all of her possessions and the very tent in which she has lived for these many years. To her we must bring our comfort and our love."

Reluctantly Miriam followed her sister-in-law, who in the bright noonday light seemed taller and much older and wiser than the black-haired wife of Benjamin. Just before they reached the tent door, Miriam put out her hand and touched Deborah upon the shoulder.

"I *am* sorry, Deborah, truly sorry for all that I have said and done in these past days. Can you forgive me—ever?"

"Come, Miriam. Let us comfort Grandmother Sarah now. It is she who needs the love of both of us."

Hours dragged on, but the Canaanites did not return, and gradually the men of Ephraim straggled back, dirty, tired, and haggard-eyed. Zelophad had never left the tent area, but he and the older men had formed a somewhat crooked line of defense in case the enemies returned.

All was quiet now. But there was a smell of smoke from the place where Asahiah's tent had been.

It was night before Benjamin and Lapidoth returned. Most of the men had already come back; three of the young men of the tribe would not return. Others had brought back their bodies for burial near the tribe.

Zelophad opened his tent to Asahiah, Sarah, Lapidoth, and Deborah. Though Asahiah was proud, he had no choice but to accept the hospitality of Zelophad.

It was with sorrow and little feasting and rejoicing that the marriage of Lapidoth and Deborah was celebrated. The whole tribe of Ephraim wondered if they would ever be able to feast or rejoice again.

Deborah herself, looking at Grandmother Sarah and then at her husband Lapidoth, wondered what in her own heart was sadness and what was joy.

Chapter 8

Asahiah the proud, a leader among the tribe of Ephraim, could not long tolerate living in the tent of another man. He began immediately to collect enough hides for a new tent.

He was a shrewd shepherd, yet well respected by his kinsmen. Always he had wanted *his* family and *his* tribe to be first among the Israelites. He had personally wanted to raise more sheep and to produce better goats than any other herdsman. Even on the hilly, rocky ground he had determined to plant and raise crops as he heard the Canaanites had done in the more fertile lands to the north.

Now his dreams were crushed and his hopes almost destroyed. In the months since his tent was destroyed, raid after raid by the Canaanites had depleted his flocks. The pile of skins for the new tent grew very slowly.

Asahiah had paced about the tent of Zelophad for days now restlessly looking here and there.

Suddenly one morning he was different—alert, excited, quick to move about.

"Lapidoth!" he called authoritatively. "Lapidoth, come here!"

Lapidoth strode quickly to his father's side, and Deborah moved instinctively to the side of the tent where she could hear the orders of this newly determined father-in-law.

"My son, prepare to move. We are going north. You and I and Grandmother Sarah and Deborah, also. We are going to move to the great valley by the River Kishon."

Other men of the tribe had gathered around now to hear Asahiah's loud announcement of his plans. If this was the plan of Asahiah, perhaps they also should think about such a move. Deborah could see Zelophad with a furrow in his brow as he rubbed the back of his hand against his chin speculatively.

"But Asahiah," warned Caleb, another of the cousins who had come to listen with amazement to this new plan, "you know how many of our people of the other tribes have been killed up there by the Canaanites."

"It makes no difference. Here we die slowly. There, perhaps, we shall find land where the river waters make things grow well. Grain I can raise there and perhaps fruit trees. You, Caleb, will see and you, too, Lapidoth and Zelophad. Surely in the north we can all become rich men!"

Lapidoth stood beside his father with a look of growing displeasure upon his face.

"You would leave our tribe of Ephraim, Father?" he asked. "It is the tribe of Manasseh who dwells by the river Kishon. They are part of the Hebrew people, but they are not of the tribe of Ephraim. How can you leave your own tribe?"

"You will be with me, Lapidoth. It will be difficult to leave our kinsmen here, but many men tell that near the cities of Taanach and Megiddo everyone becomes rich. I want to see for myself."

"Oh yes," added Caleb, "a man can indeed become rich *if* he stays alive, but few there are who can escape the raids of the Philistines or the persecution of the Canaanites in such a place. Why that area is the very capital and stronghold of the Canaanites. I must think much longer on such a daring plan as yours."

Zelophad continued to rub his chin. "I don't know. I just don't know," he repeated doubtfully.

"I shall not go with you, Father," announced Lapidoth quietly. "It is here between Ramah and Bethel that Deborah and I will dwell. You may go, Father, and the blessing of Abraham be upon you, but I shall stay here with the tribe of Ephraim."

Asahiah's own eyes shown with anger and fury at his son who had dared to disobey and stand up against his plan, but he addressed not a single word to Lapidoth. He looked around him, and about him, but never directly at his son. It was for Asahiah as if Lapidoth had ceased to exist if the son would not follow his leading.

The plan of Asahiah was no mere dream. He was a strong man and much respected among his kinsmen. If Asahiah thought that life offered more of milk and honey near Megiddo, there were those who quite naturally agreed and would follow him there. It was not long until the family of Zelophad, which included Benjamin and Miriam now, had decided to cast their lots with Asahiah.

Benjamin was much interested in the rumors that in Taanach dwelled many workers in silver and other metals. He had always been quick and skillful with his hands, and he hoped that he might gain many riches in Taanach in the metal working. How wonderful, he thought, to be able to afford silver and precious jewels to adorn the beautiful Miriam. As for Miriam, she looked forward to being adorned, so the choice for the move northward came quite naturally for these two. Zelophad, dissatisfied with life as it was in Ephraim with its uncertainties, and respecting Asahiah's judgment, became convinced that any change would be a welcome one.

Caleb's family also, after much indecision, had packed up their tent and household goods, and prepared to join the caravan moving northward.

Deborah was bitterly disappointed when her parents and Miriam and Benjamin decided to cast their lots with the tribe of Manasseh and leave the area about Mount Ephraim where they had been dwelling and moving about for so long. Always her parents had been nearby! How deeply she would miss their presence and their affection, the comradeship she had known all of her life with Benjamin, and the easy conversation with Tirzah, her mother!

She was glad for Lapidoth's decision to remain with the tribe of Ephraim, yet she wondered if she would ever again see her parents or share secrets with her brother!

With tears in her eyes she finally bid goodbye to Tirzah, and she could scarcely pull her arms away from the round body of the affectionate Huldah. Hesitantly, Deborah prepared to bid farewell to Grandmother Sarah. But with an obstinate toss of her head, the old woman belligerently sat down upon a mat and refused to move.

"I shall stay with Lapidoth and with Deborah. I will not follow the foolish dreams of that son of mine. Always Asahiah has been reckless like his father before him. No, I will not go with him. I will not watch him die in a strange place, and I shall not be buried by any River Kishon with any tribe of Manasseh. I stay here. I have lived a lifetime here, and I shall die and be buried here near Mount Ephraim."

Asahiah was annoyed and angry at his mother's obstinacy, but no one, he knew, dared change the mind of Grandmother Sarah. He continued his preparations for the journey while his mother watched him from the straw mat with marked disapproval.

Lapidoth stood beside his wife as the caravan pulled away, and tears came suddenly to Deborah's eyes as she saw Huldah turn back and wave eagerly.

"Be brave, Deborah," comforted Lapidoth, "some day we shall have our own Huldah."

Then, noting the far-off look in his wife's eyes, he added kindly, "Yes, Deborah, one day we shall have our own Simeon, also."

How lonely life would be without the laughing Huldah, and

yes, Deborah admitted to herself, even without the stern Asahiah. She was glad that she would have the snappish comfort of Grandmother Sarah.

"My wife," said Lapidoth, "I have been thinking of changes also. We are fewer in number now, and those of us left in the land of Ephraim must now work all the harder to make our tribe prosper on this land that Yahweh has given us. I have called the tribespeople together that they may hear my thinking. Prepare food and drink that they may eat before I tell them of my plans."

Later, when the people had gathered and had eaten their fill, Lapidoth began.

"Many years ago, before my father's time, and before the time of his father," Lapidoth began, "Yahweh led Joshua over the River Jordan into this land of Canaan. This land upon which we now stand was given to the people of Ephraim. My father, Asahiah, and others with him, have chosen to forsake the hills of Ephraim to dwell with the tribe of Manasseh near the River Kishon. We have chosen to stay here. For too many years our people have wandered among these hills in search of grazing land. We have lived in tents that we might quickly flee from the attacking Canaanites, and easily follow our flocks. But here, between Rahmah and Bethel beneath these palm trees, there is water and grazing land. There is land that with care and tending will yield grain from which the women will grind meal for bread. We do not need to go north to Taanach or the River Kishon, we can change our lives here in Ephraim.

Here we must abandon our tents that have served us in the days of our wanderings, and build houses that the Canaanites cannot easily burn with a flaming torch."

Proudly, Deborah listened to her husband defending his plan against the doubts and arguments of the men. One by one, she heard the men side with Lapidoth. At long last, after much discussion, she heard Lapidoth say, "So! It is decided. We shall move no more. We shall live here, beneath the palm trees, between Rahmah and Bethel!"

The house building began almost at once. The structures were small, and made of mud, but even so, there was much work involved. Within a few weeks, however, there was a small village of mud huts between Ramah and Bethel, where once there had been shepherd's tents.

Deborah and Grandmother Sarah arranged their jugs, straw mats, and bed rolls inside their new home. They took the skins apart that had been their tent and hung them so that the hut was partitioned into sleeping and eating rooms. Grandmother Sarah puttered about the new home, rearranging everything. She seemed determined to keep herself busy, but Deborah wondered how genuine was the air of cheer and nonchalance.

One day, as Deborah was taking her bread to the oven to be baked, she was stopped by the sight of two of the tribeswomen arguing heatedly and holding a kneading trough awkwardly between them. Neither would let loose from her hold on the bowl.

"What's this all about?" asked Deborah. "What can be so important that two women squabble so loud and foolishly?"

"It is *my* kneading trough, Deborah, and Rachel wants to use it all the time."

"No, it is not hers, Deborah. It was made by my grandfather, and I am the one who needs it more than this cousin of mine. Today I must bake enough loaves to last over the Sabbath rest."

"But I must bake loaves today also!" wailed Rachel's cousin.

"Bring your flour here to my tent and all of us will mix the bread and knead the dough together. All three of us can work together today, and the bread will be baked even more quickly than usual. Grandmother Sarah can even tell us stories as we knead the bread. You will see. It will work well." Deborah smiled at the two.

Both women looked at one another hesitantly, yet with less anger in their eyes than they had before.

Deborah, however, spoke again, and this time with even more sternness in her voice.

"Between the two of you, you must work out an agreement. Each of you must decide at what hours of the day you need to use this bowl.

"Be glad that you have each other to share such implements of baking. Both of you are loyal Hebrew women. You must be proud that you are of the tribe of Ephraim, and of the people of Israel. Be so proud, each of you, that you dare not grow angry with a sister, but rather save your anger and bitterness for the battle we must one day wage against our enemies!"

"How sorry we are, Deborah," they mumbled downcast.

"I had almost forgotten that Rachel was my cousin."

Together the three measured out the flour and mixed the dough. Deborah looked up at the sky with half-regret. Her own loaves would be finished baking now, and she must hurry to take them from the oven.

Deborah was stooping by the oven to remove her own loaves and set them aside to cool, when a niece of Caleb, Naomi, whose husband had not joined the northbound caravan, came rushing towards her.

"Deborah, come quickly! The baby is ill! He has become so hot and he cries constantly. He burns up with fever and I cannot get him to drink any milk."

Stopping only long enough to put aside the freshly baked loaves and to look in at Grandmother Sarah, napping on her mat in the corner of the tent, Deborah went scurrying with Naomi to look at the sick child. The baby was indeed burning up with fever.

"Quickly, Naomi, keep these cloths wet and wrap them about his body. It will help the fever to subside."

Obediently Naomi did as Deborah had indicated, and in a short time the baby softened his wails to a more gentle whimpering.

"Keep on with the wet cloths and I will go back to my tent and prepare some herbs as I have seen Tirzah do so many times. We will make your child well. He is a beautiful son, Naomi. How I wish I had one like him to care for."

Throughout the long night, Deborah and the mother, Naomi, took turns holding the infant and rocking him in their arms. The broth had helped, but he still seemed very sick.

By morning the child was improved and sleeping peacefully, but Deborah was exhausted from her sleepless night. She was fond of the small boy, but she regretted not being able to spend the quiet Sabbath evening in her own home with Lapidoth.

The women of the tribe soon came to think of Deborah whenever there was a problem to be solved. At first they were simple matters; but, as the tribespeople's respect for her judgment grew, Deborah realized that the problems brought to her were becoming of a more complicated nature.

Frequently now the leaders of the tribe came to her door with the problems of their people. Deborah's whole mind and soul was devoted to her people, but their vast worries and their great cares made her head swim with fatigue. How, she wondered, could she ever find the right answer for each person that came to her?

Indeed, for some, Deborah could find no concrete answers. She could not bring back a dead infant to a weeping mother; nor could she cause grain to grow on a field filled with stones and barren soil. But even when the obstacles were insurmountable, Deborah bestowed her compassion and understanding upon each family who sought her judgment.

There were, however, in the days and weeks that followed, sound judgments which could be meted out, and sensible solutions which could be suggested. Because of her sensitivity to their needs, Deborah was able to teach the young wives—not only a better method of saving the yeast between bakings—but a greater allegiance to Yahweh, the Lord.

To the old, Deborah listened more carefully, and her concern for their bent knees and weak eyesight gave them confidence in her youthful wisdom. In turn, they each one desired to confide in Deborah the memories and secrets and traditions of the tribe which they had cherished through the years. It was from these, the old, that Deborah learned many of the stories of Moses, and of Joshua, and of the various leaders of their own tribe of Ephraim. She learned these hero-stories, not only from the chronicles of birthrights of who begat whom, but in the songs and chants that she and Lapidoth loved so well.

One morning Deborah was standing next to the two palm trees that shaded the mud house, when suddenly she heard a noise close behind her in the bushes.

Crouched in the bushes was a young girl, her face covered with dirt. The rough tunic on her body was torn and ripped in many places.

"Come here, my child," said Deborah, motioning the girl forward.

As the disheveled figure approached, Deborah could see that the girl was older than she had first appeared. Her skin, stretched tightly over the bones of her face and shoulders, indicated that she had not eaten much in many months.

"Are you . . . are you by any chance, Deborah, the wife of Lapidoth?"

And when Deborah nodded, tears welled up in the eyes of the girl.

"Forgive my appearance," she said, "but I have been a slave of the Philistines for many months now. I am Jael of the tribe of Judah. Last year the Philistines came through our village and killed my parents. My brother and I, and others of the families who were not killed, were taken as slaves for their leaders. Just two weeks ago I was sold to a band of Canaanites who were passing through, and needed more servants for their trading journey."

As Jael continued her story, Deborah led the girl to the mud house. Inside, Deborah gave Jael water, and a bowl filled with a mixture much like stew that she had made for Lapidoth's dinner.

"Eat, Jael. Rest well, and know that you are safe here."

"I have come so far, Deborah, and I have been so frightened. When we got near the town of Bethel I was able to slip away from my Canaanite captors during the night. They surely know that I have escaped. Perhaps even now, they will be looking for me near here!"

"You will be safe here," soothed Deborah and she was certain of this protection, though she realized, too, that there was little she alone could do should the Canaanites attack.

"The Lord has led you here, Jael. We will care for you. You will not be harmed. But how did you know my name, and why did you come seeking me?"

"The morning after I had slipped away from the Canaanites near Bethel, I met an old man by the roadside who said he was Aaron the sandalmaker. When I asked him for help and a place to hide, he told me to go and seek Deborah under the palm trees between Ramah and Bethel. He said that you would remember him from your younger days, and that I would soon come to know you as a most holy woman. He promised that you would give me refuge, Deborah."

"I am not a holy woman, Jael. I am just like you or any of the other women of Israel. It is only that I love our people so dearly. Always, as I clear away a stone, or plant seeds with my husband, Lapidoth, or tend our sheep in the fields—always I say in my heart, 'This I do for my Lord, the one and Almighty Yahweh. This small thing also I do for my people of Israel!' "

"Then you *are* holy, Deborah. You must be a prophetess as the man from Bethel said. No one ever told me before that it was for such a reason that one performed their daily work."

"Rest now, Jael. If you would stay with us and be of our family, you may become as my sister and dwell here with us, for the Lord has sent you to us as a stranger and we will not turn you away."

"No. I must go on, Deborah. Before my father died, he said that I should go to Kedesh in Naphtali, and there I would find a mighty warrior, Barak, a man of lightning who would befriend me because of the service my father had one time done for his father, Abinoam."

Deborah pulled some bright colored cloth from behind the bed rolls piled in the corner. She had been saving it for clothing for the child she knew would be born within a few months.

"Here, Jael, stand tall near me so that I can measure from this cloth enough material for a new tunic for you."

"How thoughtful you are, Deborah, and how very kind!" responded the young girl, pulling herself up tall as Deborah measured the material carefully across her narrow shoulders.

Although Jael remained with her new friends, she showed little interest in the happenings of the tribe and she was constantly restless in spite of her efforts to help with the daily work. One day, Deborah found Jael crouched in a corner weeping.

"Jael, my little one. Why do you weep so? You are now one of our family."

"No, Deborah, I cannot be one of your family. I am afraid here, constantly afraid that the Canaanites will find me and kill all of us."

"Jael, dear, those particular Canaanites are gone now. You are safe here. They will not come back now after so long a time."

"But I still cannot stay. Night after night I remember the promise to my father that I would find the mighty warrior Barak, who would avenge his death. So I cannot stay, Deborah, in spite of your goodness and your kindness to me. I must go and find Barak very soon."

Seeing that her impatience was real, Deborah made inquiries in the towns of Ramah and Bethel for news of any caravan traveling northward which Jael might join for her search to

Kedesh in Napthtali. Within a few weeks a merchant from Ramah brought her word that a caravan of families from the tribe of Benjamin was traveling northward along the Jordan River at least as far as Issachar.

Immediately Deborah sent Lapidoth to Ramah to talk with the men of the caravan.

Yes, another girl could join their party. Any Hebrew girl would be welcome, they agreed, when Deborah had told them of Jael's tragic experiences with the Philistines and Canaanites.

Jael herself was delighted with the opportunity to join the caravan, and she eagerly offered to serve them in many of the household chores of the trip.

"But it is to you, Deborah, that I regret saying 'good-bye.' Never will I forget your kindness. Always I will remember your love for me and for all of our people. One day I will repay you. And every day of my life, I will pray unto Yahweh that I may find a way to serve you and to do good for our people.

"Farewell, Deborah, I will remember you!"

Deborah smiled and waved good-bye. She was certain that the faithful heart of Jael would never forget.

The days and weeks passed, and the tribespeople prospered.

The women brought to Deborah their problems of yarn-weaving and cloth dying, and the leaders also came to seek her advice on the business of all the tribe of Ephraim. Even the judges of the tribe of Ephraim sensed in Deborah a spirit of the Almighty Yahweh himself. Openly and in secret they called her "the holy woman."

As her body became larger and more awkward with the child for whom she and Lapidoth had so earnestly prayed, the mind of Deborah became more weighted with the concerns of their people. She had already become known as a "prophetess,"

a "judge" of the land, and she knew that the decisions she made with the help of Almighty Yahweh must indeed, for the sake of all the tribe of Ephraim, be wise and just in all circumstances.

But Deborah was a woman, also, and she longed for the time when her first child would be born. In eagerness Lapidoth and Deborah waited in the mud house for the signs of the birth of their firstborn.

When the time for the birth came, Grandmother Sarah was quick to assist, and Lapidoth hurriedly summoned the best midwives of the tribe. With skill and understanding the women gave help and aid to their beloved Deborah, but the skill and the help was of little use.

The child of Deborah and Lapidoth was born giving neither motion nor cry. The first son of Deborah and Lapidoth had been born—already dead.

And so Deborah saw another pile of stones erected, marking another grave. It was this pile of stones which stood between the two palm trees, near the mud house between Ramah and Bethel.

And few were the days which passed in the months that followed that Deborah did not look upon those stones and weep bitter tears for her firstborn son who had never cried.

Chapter 9

As Deborah judged on tribal matters, more serious trouble was fermenting in the north among the Canaanites and Israelites.

Attacks upon the Hebrews by the Canaanites had become more frequent, and ill prepared for battle, many Israelites died and many more were taken into slavery and captivity.

Deborah was on a hill not far from their house one morning, looking at the crops that were soon to be harvested, when she heard a commotion on the road below her.

Looking down cautiously from between some trees, Deborah could see a pitiful straggling line of slaves being whipped along the road by their Canaanite masters.

Hebrew slaves! Deborah's heart froze and her hands clenched in fury. Chains had been fastened from the hands to the feet of the slaves so that many of them could not stand erect. None could escape the chains. Few had enough strength even to make the effort, and those who had tried such a dangerous course had felt the blows of the whip across their backs till the blood had covered their bodies and their energies had been spent in the bearing of the pain.

These slaves were being taken northward, and Deborah's throat grew dry and taut in fear of what similar fate might already have come to her own parents, Asahiah, and Benjamin and Miriam. Most of all, she feared for her beloved small sister, Huldah. Deborah and Lapidoth had heard nothing from their families since the caravan had left more than two years before. Now her new concern for Jael was added to Deborah's other worries.

There had been no news from the caravan which Jael had joined, nor had Deborah expected any, but caravans moving south towards Egypt did bring word that the whole area of Naphtali was now under tremendous persecution from Jabin, the Canaanite king who lived in Hazor, just south of Kadesh.

As the slaves driven along by the Canaanite whips passed from sight, Deborah's body trembled from fear for the future of her people. And what about Jael, she wondered. Had the girl ever been able to find Barak?

Was it true, wondered Deborah, increasingly disturbed by the sight she had seen from the hills, that the Canaanites were preparing to completely destroy the Israelites as the rumors indicated? Had Jael even reached Issachar, the place where the caravan was headed? Deborah shook her head and doubted the possibility of one young girl ever getting to Kedesh and Barak. To reach there, she would have had to travel through Jabin's well-protected city of Hazor.

Slowly Deborah walked back to their mud house, with the gnawing concern for her family and for all her people growing within her heart.

Even now as she approached the palm tree, two leaders of the tribe stood waiting for her.

"There is more bad news, Deborah."

"More of our people have been murdered by the Canaanites."

"Word has come now from the north from Harosheth, which is now a haven for the Gentiles. Sisera, the vicious general of the Canaanites, has gouged out the eyes and cut off the arms and legs of many of our Hebrew people who would not serve him!"

Deborah shook her head in sadness and horror.

"The wicked king Jabin of the Canaanites must be crushed, Deborah. But how? How can we destroy our enemies?"

"You have told us, Deborah, and we have believed you, that we are the chosen people, those picked by Yahweh to rule all of Canaan. But how can we do it? How can we make such a prophecy come true?"

"It is true," said Deborah firmly, in spite of her grief, "Moses and Joshua spoke to you thus in the generations which have gone before us. Abraham also believed in this promise of Yahweh. You now, too, must believe in Almighty Yahweh that you may be victorious over our enemies. Your strength will not falter, if you trust him alone."

The leaders of the tribe shook their heads in disbelief but as Deborah continued with assurance of Yahweh's invincible strength, they looked with amazement upon the young woman who spoke about the Lord with such authority.

"Perhaps it is our faith which is lacking, Deborah."

"We have forgotten too often that we are God's chosen people!"

"We go now, therefore, Deborah, to our houses to fast and to pray."

Purposefully the men moved away from the palm trees and Deborah herself went wearily into the house to help Grandmother Sarah.

It was some days later that Deborah stood sorting some precious wheat grains to be used as seed for the next planting, when she noticed a shadow across the doorway. The shadow seemed a great, tall one.

Slowly she rose, then ran with lightning speed to throw her arms about the man in the doorway.

"Benjamin!" she cried, "Benjamin! Is it truly you? Can it possibly be that you have come back? Tell me, is it really you?"

The man was thinner and perhaps a very little taller than the brother she had known, but even with the joy of reunion, as Benjamin lifted Deborah clear from the floor in an enthusiastic embrace, there was much of worry and trouble mirrored on his face.

"Where is Miriam? And Mother and Father? And where is my wonderful Huldah?" Deborah asked in a flood of questions which poured out from her surprise and bewilderment.

"They are well, Deborah. They have their tents near the

River Kishon, and they are not far from the city of Megiddo. They are afraid there among the Canaanites, but they are well. But tell me quickly, my sister, where is Lapidoth? I have grave news for him."

"Lapidoth is out on the hills with the sheep. He has done well here, Benjamin; you would be proud of him. So well do seeds and the grain grow under his touch that all the tribe looks to him for help in the planting and harvesting."

Deborah smiled in recollection of her husband's hard and successful work, but her face grew suddenly serious again.

"What is the bad news you bring to Lapidoth?"

Benjamin turned and stood by the door.

"I must tell Lapidoth myself, Deborah. But look, could that not be him in that field beyond the palm trees?"

Deborah looked and nodded in assent, and then as if regretting his brusqueness, Benjamin turned towards his sister.

"Asahiah is dead, Deborah! You know he was never a quiet man and never could he be made to be one. It was in Megiddo one day that he insulted an officer of the army of Sisera. Immediately he was dragged away to prison. We looked for him for many days and when we finally found him, he was hanged before our very eyes.

"I must go to Lapidoth now, Deborah. There are some things a man must tell another man when he is alone."

Silently Benjamin disappeared across the fields toward the place where Lapidoth cared for the sheep.

Behind the curtains in the far room of the mud house,

Deborah heard quiet sobbing. It was Grandmother Sarah.

Swiftly Deborah went to kneel down before the old woman and to hold her shaking body against her own shoulders.

"Grandmother Sarah, all is not over! Your son will be avenged! Asahiah shall not be forgotten! I promise you this day, that such a crime *will* be punished!"

The old woman merely nodded her head in hopelessness.

Quickly Deborah stood up and took down from the wall the piece of leather strap she had carefully guarded for almost eight years now.

"Look, Sarah, see this strap. It is the piece of leather that my brother Simeon, treasured so dearly. Never have I forgotten Simeon's death by the Canaanite spear and never will I forget your son's murder either!"

Impulsively Deborah laid the strap in the hands of the old woman, and she watched the fingers tighten over the leather as if it were a final grasp of hope that she was holding upon.

"Dear Grandmother, it is not the will of Yahweh that such things come to pass. The Almighty Lord will guide and lead our people. He will teach us how our enemies can be destroyed. All my life I have prayed unto him in reverence and obedience, and he has helped me and answered the prayers for my people. Now, I will pray unto him again that the memory of Simeon and Asahiah may not be forgotten, and that our people living today may indeed be avenged for the wrongs committed against them by the Canaanites."

Moving slowly to one corner of the mud house, Deborah

fell on her knees and pulling her mantle about her face, she prayed.

When she finally arose, Deborah walked to the door of the house purposefully.

"Joshua," she called to a small neighbor boy of the tribe playing with some friends near the palm trees, "come here quickly!"

Joshua was most fond of the small honey cakes that the beloved "judge" of the tribe, Deborah, sometimes baked for the children, so he hurried to the doorway at her first call.

"This is most important, Joshua. Go now, and tell your father and the other leaders of the tribe that they are to gather here before this house of Lapidoth at sundown tonight. Each man of the tribe is to come here. Remember, now, Joshua—at sundown, tonight."

Greatly impressed by Deborah's stern manner and insistent voice, Joshua lost no time in running toward his own tent to inform his father and the other men of Ephraim.

Still standing in the doorway, Deborah could now see the two familiar but weary figures of Benjamin and Lapidoth returning.

Her husband's grief-stricken face, as he came near the house, made Deborah more sure than ever that they must now as a people stand strong and strike back against the Canaanites.

"Here, my beloved husband, and you, my dear brother, sit and rest here within the house that I may prepare your dinner for you."

Silently the men entered and sat down, but not a word

passed between them, and not a sound was uttered either by Grandmother Sarah from behind the curtain.

Deborah herself worked quickly preparing the meal, and it was not long until the thick stew was boiling.

Benjamin, as Deborah motioned him to do, went behind the curtain to Grandmother Sarah. She spoke not a word to him, but stared straight ahead, as if the final news of her son, Asahiah's death were more than she could bear and she would, therefore, close her mind to all future news either good or bad.

Benjamin spoke gently to the grandmother and kneeled down beside her so that she could see his face clearly and not be frightened. The grandmother looked directly at the man, yet she saw nothing and heard nothing either.

Deborah standing nearby, saw that she still clutched the leather strap that had been Simeon's in her hands. Benjamin, close to the grandmother, saw the strap also. With bitter grief in his eyes, he looked at Deborah, and their hearts were filled with the silent memories that neither could forget.

When the three finally sat by the straw eating mats and Deborah passed the bread, they dipped their loaves in the hot broth and pulled out the pieces of meat with their fingers, but they still found little reason to speak above the grief that had enveloped them all.

By sundown, the men of the tribe gathered before the mud house. Some leaned against the palm trees, and others sat in small groups whispering the rumors and secrets of the day.

Several of the men had seen Benjamin and the news, in its

own mysterious community-spreading manner, had indeed been passed throughout the tribe.

The burly, hot-tempered Asahiah whom they had all respected and admired—this fine man of their tribe had been murdered by the Canaanites. This, and all of the atrocities they had been enduring for years now, had suddenly and intensely become too much to bear without retaliation.

"What can we do, Deborah?" asked one of the men as she came to the doorway.

"How bad is it in Harosheth, Benjamin?" asked another as Benjamin and Lapidoth appeared also to sit among them.

"I have heard that there is terror throughout the whole city of Harosheth because of Sisera," said the husband of Rachel.

Another added, "And I have heard that in Hazor, too, the Israelites are killed by the vicious king Jabin."

"It is all true," admitted Benjamin regretfully.

"But what can we do?"

"We are not afraid to fight," cried an impetuous young man of the tribe.

An older leader sighed, "Ah yes, but it is not that easy. We have never learned the art of making war. No, we have not even learned the crafts of metal-working for making the instruments of war. As shepherds, we are not to be seconded, but as soldiers we have little hope."

It was then that Deborah stood up before them and her voice was firm.

"We have little hope because we have not tried vigorously

enough to defeat the enemy. We have let the Canaanites kill and maim and destroy our people, because we were afraid to strike back, but surely if such murder continues our people will all be slowly destroyed. We cannot much longer exist in this our Land of Canaan, if such attacks continue. Remember that it was our great Moses who once led us to the river before we entered this land, and that it was Joshua with the help of the Almighty Yahweh who guided us into this land of milk and honey. For forty years the Lord guided us up from our captivity in Egypt into this our promised land. Surely if the Lord guided us to this land, we should also defend it with our very lives. And *if* we defend it with our lives, surely also the Almighty Lord will preserve and defend us against our enemies."

As she spoke Deborah's voice had gained in strength and momentum. Not an eye moved from her face.

"How, Deborah, how?"

"*How* can we defeat the Canaanite oppressors?"

The questions came not only from Benjamin and Lapidoth but from every man among them.

Deborah herself paused, and then looking at each one before her, asked another question.

"In all of our tribes, from all of our people, who is the greatest warrior and the strongest soldier from all of Israel?"

From man after man there came a mumble and a suggestion, but the murmurs and suggestions were overwhelmingly the name of but a single man.

"Barak."

"Barak, the son of Abinoam."

"Barak from Kedesh in Naphtali, the general who had led our people in many battles in Naphtali against the evil Jabin and his Canaanite armies."

"Barak, the son of Abinoam, is stronger than any other man of our people."

"It is true. Barak is most skilled in warfare."

"Barak is the man."

With decisiveness, Deborah turned to the most light-footed and the most rapid runner of the men gathered about.

"Neheman, go." she said. "Go to Kedesh in Naphtali and summon Barak of Abinoam to come and talk with Deborah beneath the palm tree so that all of the tribes of Israel may know peace once more."

As the runner departed, the man began to turn and talk with one another in sudden eagerness and anticipation.

As they talked among themselves, few saw Deborah slip alone into the house. Within her own walls, Deborah sat down upon a straw mat and bent her head upon her knees.

The death of Simeon, the murder of Asahiah, the oppression of all the children of Israel by the Canaanites—all of it suddenly seemed too much for her to bear.

The people of Ephraim might call her a "judge" or a "holy one," but tonight, alone in her house, she was only a woman, very, very weary from the shocks and disappointments of the day.

Chapter 10

Around the mud house of Deborah and Lapidoth, many tents had been set up. Soldiers bustled about in the assembling of what seemed almost a military encampment.

Outside the house of Deborah were the noises of the fastening down of tents, the preparing of food and the drawing of water from the nearby well. Inside the house there was no bustling and for many moments there was little conversation.

The light from three oil lamps cast shadows in the early evening, as a powerful man and a strong woman faced each other across the straw mat on which lay raisins, dates, and small honey cakes.

The eyes of Deborah were calm as she drew the red and gold shawl which had been Grandmother Sarah's wedding gift, about her head and shoulders.

So this is the mighty Barak, son of Abinoam, she thought. Is he really as strong as I have heard reported? Is he brave and strong enough to lead all of our people against the hosts of Jabin and Sisera? I wonder.

But not a word passed her lips as she offered to Barak more of the honey cakes and figs.

As Benjamin and Lapidoth sat silently in the shadows, Barak looked at Deborah. Disappointment was written on his face. He seemed to be asking silently, "Why have I traveled so far to see this woman? Why have I brought my soldiers on so long a journey to meet with this Deborah who looks not very different from every other woman I have met?"

Deborah sensed Barak's annoyance at being summoned by a mere woman.

Quietly and decisively she spoke to his irritability.

"It is not I who have called you here, mighty Barak, son of Abinoam. It is the Lord God of Israel who has called you forth and brought you here that our people may be saved!"

Barak looked sharply at Deborah.

How dared a woman speak in such a manner! He had never before heard anyone, much less a woman, speak with such firmness and such authority.

"Our people are being oppressed. Hebrew men and women are being killed by Jabin, and by his captain, the evil Sisera. Our own homes are being destroyed by these Canaanites. We are not safe upon the highways of our country. We cannot walk in freedom upon this land given us by Yahweh. If we do not act now, all of Israel will be destroyed forever."

Barak nodded silently.

This had also been his secret fear—the slow destruction of Israel by the Canaanites, yet never had he thought that he would hear such words from a Hebrew woman. It was extremely annoying to think that a woman would come to the same conclusion as he, the mighty Barak.

"I am afraid that what you say is true, Deborah."

The "judge" of the Hebrews was watching him carefully and he squirmed beneath her scrutiny.

"But what can we do about it, even if such things are true?"

"You could do something."

"What can I do against all the power of the Canaanite armies?"

"You are the strongest warrior in all of Israel, are you not, Barak?"

Barak nodded. "I *am* strong," he affirmed.

"And do you not love your people of Naphtali? Would you not serve all of our people of Israel? Did not the Lord God lead us up out of Egypt and through the wilderness for forty years that we might come to this land where no people should drive us out nor conquer nor oppress us?"

Again Barak nodded in agreement.

Persistently Deborah held to her advantage.

"The Lord has done all these things for you. Will you not then do something for your people? Would you let your people be destroyed, as you sit by like a meek lamb or a quivering coward?"

Barak sprang to his feet.

"How dare you ask such a question? How dare you question the loyalty of the captain of the soldiers of all Kadesh-Naphtali? Woman of Ephraim, do you not know that I have already spent twenty years of my life fighting for our people?"

There was the trace of a smile on the lips of Deborah. She had not only aroused the anger, but the interest also of the mighty warrior. The rest, she reasoned, should not be so difficult.

Deborah rose and moved slowly towards Barak, then stooped and poured more goats' milk from the skin beside them. Gracefully drawing the folds of the red and gold mantle about her shoulders, Deborah sat down again calmly, but the light from the oil lamp showed her brown eyes sparkling and glowing from the excitement of her plan.

"For many days I have prayed here by the palm tree that the Almighty Yahweh would show me a way to save our people."

Barak was now listening intently and for the first time his voice had lost its tone of condescension.

"I have prayed for our people, also, Deborah. Tell me, then, what *can* I do?"

"This is not my plan, Barak, it is the work of the Lord. For days I prayed unto him to show me the way, and this is the plan which he has revealed to me."

Barak shook his head almost doubtfully.

"I don't understand. It is too strange for me. I have prayed unto the Lord also, but he has never spoken to me nor revealed a plan to me, the greatest of his warriors. Why would he speak to you, a woman, when he has not spoken to me?"

"I do not know, Barak. I only know the words that the Lord spoke to me. In a dream last night he revealed his plan for our people. It is true, Barak, that you, alone, cannot save Israel—nor can I. Yet you, son of Abinoam, can help in the victory of Israel over her enemies."

"Go on, I am listening."

"Barak, it is you who must summon all the tribes to call forth their best warriors that together, as one united people of Israel, we can attack and conquer these Canaanites forever."

Barak's great eyebrows furrowed together.

"Maybe they won't listen to me."

"They will listen to the Lord, Barak. It is he who will speak through you, his warrior of Kedesh-Naphtali."

Barak paced the floor.

"I don't know. There are too many details to consider."

"It was Yahweh who spoke to me, Barak, and said that if all the forces of all the tribes should be gathered together at Mount Tabor, we should be ten thousand strong."

"At Mount Tabor?"

He had been there often. Strange, Barak thought, that he should not have worked out such a plan himself. Mount Tabor was in the center of all the Canaanite trouble, and it was most certainly an excellent spot for a such a strategic military maneuver. Yes, it was a good plan, even for a woman. Already his mind, accustomed to the practices of warfare, was warming to the scheme.

"But the tribes would have to be notified," he insisted

brusquely, "and time must be given for the soldiers to purify themselves. Runners ought to be sent immediately to notify all of our people."

Deborah poured more oil for the lamps.

She was delighted. Barak had indeed been captured by the idea of a Canaanite defeat!

Barak then laughed shrewdly.

"Oh, yes, Sisera will lead his army to the Kishon River without a doubt. Many are the Canaanite spies already circulating about, and it will not be difficult to lure Jabin's army toward Mount Tabor."

Suddenly, however, Barak's smile faded and his face became stern.

"But I will not go alone, Deborah. This has been your plan. It was to you that the Lord spoke and not to me."

Deborah paused uncertainly. She had been so sure that Barak was convinced of the plan, and it troubled her greatly now to see the soldier's face so dark with determination.

"I will go, Deborah. I will risk my life and the life of the men in my army, but I will not go alone. If you will go with me, I shall go, but if you will not go with me, then I am through with this plan. I shall go back to Kedesh and forget that I ever met such a woman as Deborah, and I shall never lead a single man towards Mount Tabor."

"Me—go with you into battle? Why, I know nothing about warfare! Whoever heard of a woman going to war?"

Barak was adamant.

"Whoever heard of a woman planning a battle either? My mind is made up. If you go with me, I will go. If you will not go with me, I will not go."

A thousand thoughts now jumbled themselves in the mind of Deborah. She had thought her mission accomplished—merely to tell the plan to Barak. She *had* convinced him that the maneuver was indeed a good one. Surely, this was enough, Deborah thought, and secretly hoped that Yahweh would speak also to Barak that he might go forth leading the army alone.

Hastily she looked towards her husband, Lapidoth, sitting silently with Benjamin in the shadows.

How could she leave Lapidoth even for a few months? How could she leave this home she loved so dearly? She was not a soldier. She was only a woman who wanted to live quietly.

Barak rose and strode deliberately towards the door.

"Think well tonight, Deborah. I shall wait until morning for your answer. Remember that it was *you* who asked *me* if I loved Israel. How about you, Deborah? How much do the Hebrew people mean to you?"

Deborah rose as if to answer, but already Barak had disappeared toward his tent far on the other side of the palm tree.

Chapter 11

Never in all of her life had Deborah remembered being so tired. Her body ached from the long hours and weary days of travel with the soldiers of Barak. Her mind was jumbled with the plans of battle, and it now seemed as if years had passed since the Lord had spoken to her so clearly in the house beside the palm tree.

Those had been more comfortable days—the time of love and joy with her husband, Lapidoth, and their happiness in the simple chores of growing the grain and the solving of problems for her own family and her own tribespeople. Yet Deborah knew that she must now ride into battle with all of Israel—this was her responsibility, her holy duty. The Lord had spoken unto her, unto her Yahweh had revealed his plans, and so now, it was she, Deborah, who must lead them into this war for their people and for their Lord.

If God had spoken directly to Barak, Deborah would have been able to stay at the mud house, but the Lord had not revealed his plans to the son of Abinoam but to Deborah, a daughter of the tribe of Ephraim. In spite of the heat, the fatigue, the loneliness without her husband, Deborah knew that her decision could have been none other than the leading of the armies against Canaan.

The slow journey gave her time to remember many things. She could not forget her childhood days—the childhood fall which had stiffened her ankle and the holy moments when the family had first made the trip to Shechem to worship in the tabernacle. It seemed to Deborah, as she looked back, that through each of these days, and each of her childhood experiences, her love for the Lord and her devotion to Israel had grown slowly and consistently, even as she herself had developed from a child into a mature woman.

The bitterness she had felt at the death of Simeon, however, would never leave her mind, and she knew it was the loss of her brother as well as the death of Asahiah and the oppression of all the Hebrews which indeed had made her decision imperative. She could never forsake her people nor the memory of Simeon.

After all the slow and growing years, Deborah realized that now she was finally able to *do* something for Israel, but her feelings suddenly puzzled her. Her back ached, her eyes burned from the dust of the road, and her throat was dry from the long, tedious journey. She didn't feel one bit like a "judge," nor even the least like a patriot. She felt merely like a woman lonesome for her husband and weary for her home.

Lapidoth had not been surprised by Deborah's decision. He

knew well her tremendous love for Israel and the respect in which she was held in her own tribe. He knew she could do nothing else than accept the challenge which the Lord held before her. Lapidoth loved his people also, but he knew that his part now was not as a leader. He longed most of all to grow good grain and to become even a better singer of the songs and stories of their Hebrew people. Lapidoth would have been content to remain forever in the house by the palm tree between Ramah and Bethel.

Now he could not.

If his wife was to lead all of the tribes, at least he must stir up enthusiasm for the plan among his own people.

He and Benjamin had left the mud house even before Deborah had gathered her belongings together for her journey northward. Benjamin, it was arranged, would go back to his wife and mother and father whom he hoped still lived in the tents near Megiddo. On the way he would issue the call to arms to the tribe of Manasseh, and then later to the tribe of Zebulon.

Lapidoth, after traveling throughout Ephraim to enlist men to fight, would then head southward to inform the leaders of the tribe of Benjamin of their plans.

Deborah, therefore, her donkey moving slowly towards Kedesh, knew that the mud house now stood empty. Grandmother Sarah had not spoken a word since she heard of the murder of her son, Asahiah, but sat silently in her own corner of Rachel's house wrapped in her thoughts and memories of other happier years. Before Deborah left, Rachel had come and gently led the grandmother to her own house. The aged were always to be well respected, and none in the tribe would ever allow the mother of Asahiah to be in need. It was thus that the grandmother had gone from the house . . . and Lapidoth . . . and Deborah.

Deborah wondered now if she and Lapidoth would ever again plant seeds in their fields, tell stories near the palm trees for a wedding feast, or fill the lamps with oil inside the mud house and sit together in contentment and security. Such happiness with Lapidoth, Deborah thought, was indeed the greatest hope of her life now!

But, no! Deborah straightened her back. That wasn't her greatest hope, after all, or she wouldn't be traveling here north of the Sea of Chinnereth so many, many miles from Ramah. Her greatest dream was not for herself, not even for Lapidoth, but for every one of the thousands of her people that they might be free of enemies and oppressors and that they might live in peace in the land of Canaan which the Lord had given them. Such hope, she was convinced, could never die, could never be changed.

Barak was now signaling the caravan to stop, and indeed they were a caravan with the soldiers, tents, donkeys, equipment and two women—Deborah and the young woman Hannah, who had accompanied her as a companion for the journey.

"We will make camp here," announced Barak in a stentorian voice, indicating a level place to the left of the road. "I am familiar with the land now, and there is a well here that can give water for us and for our horses."

Deborah was more than willing to stop, though the land appeared to offer little of hospitality and comfort. Other nights had been better, for one evening they had camped beside the Sea of Chinnereth. The sunset had been fantastically beautiful, and Deborah thought she had never been more homesick for the land between Ramah and Bethel. Here by the slopes of Mount Tabor they would wait for the other soldiers to join them.

As always, Barak was right about the watering place. He was not a man with a cheerful or friendly nature, but he possessed an uncanny knowledge of the land—where water might be found, where encampment would be most safe. He was even more certain of his directions now as they entered the region near Naphtali which was home for him.

It was not long until the soldiers had pounded the pegs into the ground to fasten the tent of Deborah and Hannah securely. As Deborah waited for the skins to be stretched more tightly across the frame, she motioned for Hannah to come and walk with her to the well that they could now see at the edge of the encampment. The well was important, for every military encampment must be kept ritually clean and each soldier must perform exact and precise rules of cleanliness.

"It will be good to drink here and to save some of the water in the jugs for washing ourselves later. Surely, Hannah, in Ramah the dust was not so sticky as it is here in Naphtali, or have I just forgotten?"

The young companion smiled.

"Perhaps, good Deborah," she replied, it is only we who have become more sticky and more covered with dust."

Deborah put her arm lightly on the shoulders of Hannah. "Perhaps we are both right."

They walked on for a few moments in silence, glad of the chance to be down from the horses and to stretch their legs before nightfall.

"Look, Hannah, there is another woman drawing water from the well. Maybe we can find out from her just how far it is to Kedesh without bothering Barak. He seems in a particularly gruff mood today."

The woman had been bending over the well, but as she raised her head and saw Deborah and the girl approaching, her eyes grew wide, first in amazement and then in fear.

Suddenly Deborah began to run towards the well, but the woman, with her water jug clutched in one arm, held a finger to her own lips as if signifying silence. Deborah could see the fear, almost terror, in the eyes behind the upheld finger, so she stopped her quick advance to the well.

The woman, with a silent motion that was almost like the throwing of a kiss in the direction of Deborah, turned and darted across the road. Deborah watched her make her way to a tent made from camel skins that sprawled in an ungainly manner over the ground and before the tent Deborah could see a small dark man watching them with keen and wily interest.

"Hannah, did you see that woman at the well? It was Jael, I know it was, but I just can't believe my eyes."

"It did look like Jael, Deborah, but it has been a year since she left us, we could be mistaken."

"It was Jael. I am sure of it. I could never forget Jael."

"She seemed terribly frightened, Deborah. And why wouldn't she have welcomed you with open arms?"

"It is very strange, but didn't you notice the man who watched so suspiciously in front of the tent door where she carried back the water?"

"If that was Jael, she seemed so afraid that it almost frightens me, Deborah. Come on, now, though, let me draw some water for both of us, so we can get back to our own tent. Barak will be sending a soldier out looking for us, if we don't hurry back."

Deborah walked back to the tent in silence. It *had* been Jael, she was certain. She could never forget the face of the young girl whom she had come to love even as a younger sister.

Had Jael forgotten? It had been little more than a year ago that Jael had promised *never* to forget Deborah, and to one day show her love and gratitude. Deborah could not understand it: here, today, when coming almost face to face, Jael had seemed not even to recognize her.

So deeply was Deborah engrossed in her own thoughts that she scarcely heard Barak approach.

"Deborah, we must make more plans for the purifying of the soldiers before the battle. We ought soon to hear from the tribes how many men they will send to fight with us against the Canaanites. Naphtali and Zebulun have already gathered up their strongest from all the families of their tribes. We ought to hear now from the others, if we are to number ten thousand in our march to Mount Tabor.

"Barak, who does that awkward sprawling tent on the other side of the road belong to? Do you know?"

Barak furrowed his brow, then raised his finger in recall.

"Oh, that one!" and he spat upon the ground. "That tent belongs to Heber the Kenite. So treacherous was he with his own tribe that he left the Kenites and now wanders from place to place."

Suddenly Barak was more serious.

"Yet he is not to be taken lightly. One day he will come to sell information to me about the camp of Sisera, but I know all the time that next week he will run to Sisera or Jabin about my plans. A spy he is. He spies on everything and everyone and is to be trusted by no one. But what made you notice his tent? What made you even ask about it?"

"I saw a woman at the well, Barak, and she took her jug of water into this tent. I'm sure I know the woman, but while Heber watched us she gave no sign of welcome or recognition."

"It could have been Heber's wife. I do not know her, but many people are justly afraid of that treacherous Kenite and perhaps she is also."

Deborah was not satisfied, for to her Jael was vastly more important than Barak's comments about Heber. Her thoughts, however, were interrupted as both she and Barak looked to the south and suddenly saw one of their runners making his way haltingly towards the camp.

"Here, get a rug for this man to lie upon and some water that he may drink," Barak sternly ordered two young soldiers standing in conversation nearby.

"Deborah. Barak. I have news for you," panted the runner coming near the tent now.

"The news will wait," answered Deborah comfortingly as she wondered if Lapidoth were similarly exhausted from his mission to the tribes.

"Bring this man to my tent immediately," Barak ordered, "and see that he has refreshment and that his needs are cared for there."

Barak strode to his tent as Deborah and her companion, Hannah, followed close behind.

What would the news be? How would it help their plans? Or would it help at all? Deborah's mind was bursting with questions.

The runner gained back his breath and strength as he drank haltingly from the jug of water handed to him and reached for a piece of the scarce fruit that the aides of Barak had brought out and set before him.

"The news I have brought will not bring you joy," said Joachim, the runner, leaning upon one elbow on the rug of Barak. "Many days have I traveled seeking men to fight together in the tribes of Reuben and Gilead."

Deborah leaned forward in anticipation. Yes, now she recognized this man as one who had left their house immediately after her decision to go with Barak into battle.

"How bad is the news, Joachim?" asked Barak soberly. It was better to know that they could count on but a few hundred men from the tribes of Reuben and Gilead than to expect two thousand later.

"How many *will* they send us?" pressed Deborah.

The young man shook his head.

"None," he answered.

"None!" roared Barak. "Surely you are mistaken! Surely you joke or have forgotten the number in your long trip!"

Joachim again shook his head.

"I traveled to the east from Ramah and cross the great river where it empties into the Sea of Salt. Quickly I journeyed through all the tribe of Reuben, talking to the captains of the soldiers there.

"With every family the answer was the same. With every leader, I received good food and comfortable lodging, but no offer of help. The Canaanites do not attack east of the Jordan River. For the tribe of Reuben there are many problems with the Philistines, but they see no reason to fight the Canaanites. For them Mount Tabor is too far away. They will no nothing."

"Well, perhaps the tribe of Reuben is too far south, but what of the men of Gilead? Certainly some of them will help us."

"No," answered Joachim, "not a one."

"The tribe of Gilead," he continued, "does lie north of Reuben, but most of the families are further east. I spoke with the leaders at their tents near Jogbehah, south of the River Jabbok. They sent greetings and good wishes for victory over our enemies, but the Canaanites were not their concern. They sent songs for us to sing when we would triumph over the Canaanites, but not a single man."

Barak strode angrily back and forth within the tent.

"Songs and good wishes, what good are these? Will they destroy the chariots of the Canaanites or burn down the palace of Sisera?"

Deborah's shoulders drooped and she pulled her red and gold mantle about her face to hide the diasppointment mirrored there.

"I will go to my own tent, Barak. No victory can I gain here. In my own tent I will pray to Yahweh. Surely the Lord will help us. He cannot fail us now when we are carrying out his own instructions."

Deborah and Hannah slipped from the tent of Barak and made their way to their own sleeping quarters.

"Is this the end?" Deborah asked of Hannah. "Are all our efforts and sacrifices to mean nothing? How can we win the battle without help?"

In the corner of her tent, crushed by Joachim's news of failures, and exhausted from her own long journey, Deborah kneeled down to pray.

As darkness fell, Hannah spread out the straw mat near Deborah and placed wheat cakes and goat's milk on the flat table so that her companion might have nourishment, but for many hours Deborah did not drink from the milk nor eat of the bread.

Hannah, having long before satisfied her own thirst and hunger, had lain down and almost fallen asleep when Deborah finally arose from her prayers.

Her companion almost gasped with astonishment, for although Deborah had not slept nor eaten, her face was radiant and she walked with assurance and purpose.

"Come, Hannah," she said, "we are going to the tent of Barak to talk of plans of victory for our people."

Bewildered by her complete change of attitude, Hannah followed Deborah past the tents of the many sleeping soldiers.

"Barak! Barak! Wake up!" called Deborah as she stood by the captain's tent.

"Wake up?" growled a voice from within. "Who could sleep on a night of such failure and despair?"

Deborah and Hannah entered the tent and saw Barak sitting upon the rug, brooding in the half-darkness, as the light from the oil lamp flickered hesitantly.

"Rise! Rise up, Barak! It is not a night of failure, but one of joy and victory! We shall conquer the Canaanites. Indeed, we shall destroy all of them in a single battle!"

"Victory? What wild talk do you have of victory, Deborah? You do not even know the worst yet. My soldiers have now come back from the tribe of Dan also. There on the seacoast of the Great Sea, would you not think that many would rise to fight with us?"

Barak paused for emphasis.

"Not a one will help us. It is just like Joachim's report from Reuben and Gilead. The tribe of Dan is busy fighting the Philistines, and they are being attacked by the Sea People, as well. They have their own enemies to conquer, and they will not join us in our battle. Why, therefore, do you come, Deborah? There are no plans, no battles to be fought, no victories for our people!"

Despairingly the mighty Barak buried his face in his strong arms.

"You are wrong, Barak, you are wrong!" answered Deborah confidently. "There *is* joy! There *is* cause for shouting! Victory *will* be ours! Of this I am most certain."

"Certain? How can you be certain of anything but failure? I have given you nothing but news of defeat. Why did I ever listen to you in the first place, Deborah? It all started in that mud house of yours, and under that confounded palm tree. I wish I had never heard of you nor your plans, no, not even of your town of Ramah and Bethel!"

Hopelessly Barak turned his back on the women and held his head in his hands.

"The Lord has spoken to me, Barak."

"But the Lord spoke to you before, Deborah, and look at us now! Already we are defeated!"

"No, Barak, we are not defeated. How can we be defeated when we have not yet fought? The Lord has promised us victory. We *shall* have ten thousand men at Mount Tabor, and we *shall* slay every one of the Canaanites who come out against us.

But you cannot do it by sitting here within your tent weeping. Up! Rise up, mighty Barak, son of Abinoam, it is for you to lead your armies!"

Barak stared at Deborah with vast impatience.

"You!" he said, "you will not let me mourn in peace!"

"But you can do it, Barak. We can have victory with Yahweh leading us against our enemies. If you just will not give up, Barak, we *can* do it."

"Very well, Deborah," said Barak wearily; "I will not yet give up the plan. Some way, those men I have now will be ready for battle. It is true that I can do no more; yet for the Lord I can surely do no less."

"I am proud of your courage, Barak. You will see. Victory *will* come. Yet of this one thing I must warn you. This the Lord has spoken to me that the honor of this journey shall not be thine, for the Lord will give Sisera into the hand of a woman."

"Even that doesn't matter. Nothing matters but victory. But a woman, Deborah, how very strange. Why would the Lord do this? And who will this woman be? Will you be the woman who slays Sisera, Deborah?"

"No," answered Deborah, "the woman is not me. I do not know her name."

Chapter 12

"When you go forth to war against your enemies, and see horses and chariots and an army larger than your own, you shall not be afraid of them, for the Lord your God is with you, who brought you up out of the land of Egypt."

Loudly Deborah called out the words to the army spread out below her on the southern slopes of Mount Tabor. She shivered as the rain drenched her clothes with its steadiness and persistence.

Would the men lose their enthusiasm for the battle in the damp and dismal greyness of the day? Or would they forget themselves and their present discomfort in their tremendous love for Israel? How fervently Deborah hoped they could forget the storm!

"Awake! Awake!" she cried. "Rise and defeat the enemies of our people. Stand up now, and slay the Canaanites, that the Lord God of hosts may be with you!"

Deborah looked down upon the troops spread out before her. How could they have assembled so many men? Even without the tribes of Reuben, Dan, and Gilead, they had been able to enlist these soldiers, ten thousand men of Israel who now stood before her ready to fight and ready to die for Yahweh and Israel!

On her left Deborah could see the men from Ephraim, Benjamin, Issachar and Manasseh, and among these soldiers she knew that one was more dear to her than all the others. Lapidoth, her husband, was somewhere in the hazy, rain-drenched army before her. She tried to pick out his familiar figure but the rain clouded her vision, and in the morning fog, the men and tents all seemed to be mingled together.

In front of her and to her right ranged the tribes with the greatest troops of all. From Zebulun and Naphtali had come eight thousand men. Their lives and the lives of their families were in jeopardy as they took up their arms to be led into battle, yet they knew that their land and their homes were in even greater danger had they not responded to the call of Barak and Deborah.

Shaking back her wet cloak and with her dark hair bared to the rain, in a manner uncommon to Hebrew women, Deborah walked forward to a higher ledge that her voice might be heard more clearly.

"Hear, O Israel . . ." she shouted with a voice triumphant with the hope of victory, and her voice was echoed by every man from every tribe till the words became as a refrain, "Hear, O Israel . . . Hear, O Israel . . . O Israel . . . Hear . . . Hear, O Israel!"

Strongly, firmly, authoritatively Deborah admonished the soldiers, as a priest of Israel had done the Hebrew armies in all of the past decades. She used the same words, and yet for the first time, it was no man speaking, no priest admonishing the soldiers. In all of Israel's history for the first time it was a woman leading the tribes to battle!

Courageously Deborah shouted to her beloved Hebrews, "Hear, O Israel, you draw near this day to battle against your enemies: let not your heart faint; do not fear or tremble or be in dread of them; for the LORD your God is he that goes with you, to fight for you against your enemies, to give you the victory!"

And through the lines of the troops came back the echoes, "Fight against your enemies . . . fight . . . the Lord goes with you . . . victory . . . victory . . . victory!"

Close behind Deborah stood Barak. His brow had even more than its usual furrows. This rain bothered and bewildered him.

He knew well that Sisera's army was camped on the other side of the River Kishon. He was certain that the Canaanites would have done nothing on such a day as this with rain drenching the land and torrents of water flooding the Kishon.

They themselves could have had another day of preparation here by Mount Tabor were it not for Deborah. Deborah. This uncanny woman had wakened him before dawn. There standing before his tent, already dressed in her clothes for battle, she had ordered him up and into the fray. It was almost too bewildering to comprehend.

"Up, Barak," she had said. "This is the day in which the Lord has given Sisera into your hand. Does not the Lord go out before you?"

Even now, Barak was not entirely certain that this *was* the day for a battle. He and the ten thousand men before him were already soaked and chilled.

Strange though, he thought, they seem not even to feel the rain or the cold. They can only hear Deborah's voice. That woman! Fantastically enough, she even makes *me* feel brave enough to face all of Sisera's chariots!

Barak knew well that there were nine hundred chariots of iron ranged against them along the Kishon encampment. Sisera, when he heard rumors of the Hebrews' strength, had summoned all his troops also, and they had been swift in riding down from the Canaanite stronghold at Harosheth.

Rumors indeed, grumbled Barak to himself, that wretched Heber the Kenite was seen spying too often in both camps. It was obvious that Sisera had paid him much for the information about the Hebrew army.

Barak knew all about it. Did he not have friends of his own who brought him news about the iron chariots and the heavy armor of the Canaanite soldiers? Heber, himself sold Barak much information, if the price were right.

There was no time now for pondering the rumors.

Deborah had issued the battle cry, and now swiftly Deborah and Barak must go before the troops, leading them to the River Kishon and the armed but unsuspecting Canaanites.

There was little precision in the marching of the Israelites. These were not the carefully trained and well-equipped soldiers of Sisera, but shepherds from Ephraim and fishermen from Issachar, men from Zebulun and Naphtali working on small farms with unhandy implements. The implements of sheep-herding, of fishing and of farming were familiar to these soldiers but the implements of war which they carried now so awkwardly were most strange companions.

The Israelites scarcely looked or acted or marched like soldiers, but with the coercing and praising, the ordering and the cajoling of Deborah, they had begun to *think* like soldiers.

Deborah, with her mighty spirit of patriotism, had indeed convinced them that this *was* a war into which they were being led by Yahweh. The Lord would *not* forsake them! The Lord *would* guide them! The Almighty God of Hosts *would* give them victory for their people!

The rain now beat down upon them and straggled their marching lines, but it did not make them tremble. It was not only Deborah and Barak going before them. It was indeed the Lord of Hosts leading them to victory!

The Canaanites across the Kishon did not long remain unsuspecting. Ten thousand men were marching down upon them. Sisera cursed the weather and screamed orders to his captains to harness the horses to the chariots!

Ten thousand men—he spat upon a chariot wheel! These sheep-herders would be defeated before this day was past!

They were merely straggling shepherds meandering against the force of his own army, trained for years and outfitted in the heaviest of armor. On any other day he would have laughed at the very thought of such a trifling straggling attempt. Today it annoyed him, infuriated him!

Each of his men carried a spear strong and hefty enough to cut down a dozen Israelites. His nine hundred chariots would *plow* through the forces of the Israelites. Those stupid Hebrews! They never were very smart anyhow, expecting that God of theirs to lead them to some kind of victory! The gods of Canaan were stronger than Yahweh. Indeed the gods of Canaan would protect Sisera's army!

"On, men!" barked Sisera, "let's slay those shepherds with the backs of our swords and knock them over with our shields. Cut them down quickly, and there'll be much of the bounty and spoils from all their tribes to carry back to Harosheth tomorrow. Let's slay them today, and tomorrow we may grab up the spoils!"

"Fight well and there'll be a woman slave of the Israelites for every man to carry back to Harosheth with him. And the bounty—you can pick for yourselves. Men, when the battle is over—dyed work and embroidered cloths—dyed work with embroidery for all of you! You can have your pick from all their tents and all their tribes! Waste no time! Climb now into your chariots and charge against Israel! Line up those horses and we'll go to meet those invaders on the other side of the Kishon!"

Sisera mounted into his own chariot and lashed at the two horses before him with his whip.

"Those stupid fools . . . on a miserable, wretched day like this, to try to attack all the Canaanite army. But I'll show them and their little God. We'll slay them to a man. Yes, every man and that woman also, that accursed judge of Ramah and Bethel. Let *her* feel the sword of the Canaanite also. She'll be lying dead, too, before this battle is over!"

Sisera listened. Already he could hear the chanting of the Hebrews on the road from Mount Tabor to the Kishon.

By now the Canaanite chariots and horsemen ranged in precise lines.

The foot soldiers stood at attention.

Swords gleamed and spears were held ready.

Still the rain poured down upon their feathered helmets and ran off their armor.

"Charge!" cried Sisera. "Charge for Canaan!"

"On across the Kishon! Look, on across the river! I can already see their puny soldiers!"

"On chariots and horsemen! On soldiers and spear-throwers! On to a victory for Canaan!"

Already the river Kishon had overflowed its banks. Already the torrents of rain made deep mud holes in the bank.

On the other side of the river, the soldiers of Deborah felt the mud sticking to their feet also, but the torrents of rain seemed only to make them shout more triumphantly of victory!

The Hebrews were by the Kishon now, and the heart of

Barak knew great terror as he saw dimly the mighty Canaanite chariots approaching the banks to plow down upon the army of Israel.

Deborah watched with less fear, but with the sharpest eyes of all.

"Look, Barak, look! The Lord *is* delivering us! Look at the chariots! Look at the horses sink into the mud!"

On rushed both armies now—straight for the river—straight for the slaying of one another! Loud were the shouts! Terrorized were the screams! Canaanite spears were hurled across the water!

With their swords ready and their shields before them against the approaching soldiers of Israel, the Canaanites suddenly moved no farther. From the Kishon banks the army of Sisera tried to lunge forward, but they could make no advance.

Again and again they tried to lunge forward.

Again and again they fell back.

Sisera lashed more furiously at his horses with the whip.

"On, fools! On for the victory of Canaan!"

But the more he lashed at the horses, the deeper sank the wheels of the chariots in the mud. Horsemen dashed forward, but the galloping of horses ceased as the animals frantically tried to lift their legs from the enclosing muck of the overflowing river. Soldiers desperately leaped from their animals, but their slowness gave the foot soldiers of the Israelites time to reach them first.

Loud were the screams! Terrified were the shouts as one chariot after another sank into the deep mud ruts.

Barak himself leaped from his horse and with the swarm of his men forded the river, shouting their victory cry!

It was Sisera for Barak! Sisera was the prize he wanted! Sisera would die by Barak's own hand!

There was the Canaanite captain close before him, there in his own chariot, firmly entrenched in the mud! The fierce lashing of the whips on the horses made the iron wheels sink more deeply each minute.

Sisera was bewildered. Those be-deviled Israelites! There . . . there before him was that crafty Barak! But he'd not get Sisera! Never would Sisera die at the hand of an Israelite!

Leaping down from his chariot, Sisera furtively darted among his men and the worthless chariots. On foot Sisera ran away from the battle, from Barak and from the River Kishon!

Barak watched Sisera spring down and the Israelite tried to rush towards the chariot, but no man could hurry in the mud of the river. In an instant Sisera was lost from view.

Deborah herself was almost trampled by the wild maze of mud and rain, of tramping horses and shouting soldiers being carried away by the rushing torrent of the River Kishon which had now become a mighty sea sweeping men and horses wildly away in its currents.

Screams of death! Shrieks of terror! All these rose up from the mud as flashing swords cut down the Canaanites, unnerved and ill-prepared without their chariots and horses!

Shouting commands and cries of courage to her people, Deborah watched the hand-to-hand combat of the men. Chariots had been left mired in the rut and horses had been abandoned.

Man met man. Soldier fought against soldier upon the banks. Spear was hurled against spear, and swords did their deadly vengeance.

Two men charged at one another in the mud and Deborah caught sight of a familiar face. Beneath the mud and through the rain, even then she knew she could not mistake Lapidoth. She saw a spear lifted in the air, but as she darted towards the place, other soldiers rushed before her against other enemies. A horse bucked and she avoided its frantic, pawing hoofs, but in the seconds of confusion, she had lost sight of Lapidoth. Frantically, she searched among the mud-covered soldiers, but no single man could be discovered in the swarming mass.

Gradually the charge diminished, and gradually the torrents of rain ceased to pour down. Barak could now see the few fleeing Canaanites and he, with a hundred or more of the Israelites, sped after them on foot.

Along the sides of the River Kishon they pursued the enemy.

Many were the Canaanites who fell by the banks and were carried away by the onrushing torrents, for their heavy armor weighted them too heavily for swimming or escape. Many more also were the soldiers of the Canaanites who died at the hands of the pursuing Israelites as the Hebrews followed them even as far as Sisera's own camp at Harosheth.

Barak was swift in his searching for the Canaanites, but where had Sisera hidden himself? Where had the Canaanite captain fled?

Barak was determined to slay the leader of the enemy himself!

All the way to Harosheth Barak traveled after his quarry, but never once did he catch a glimpse of Sisera.

Confound it! Surely Deborah's prophecy would not be right! Surely he would soon be able to pull out his sword and himself cut down this most dangerous of all his enemies!

Chapter 13

It was a strange reunion of deep and mixed emotions when Deborah finally reached the tent of Zelophad and Tirzah the morning after the terrible battle of the Kishon.

Great was Deborah's joy at seeing again her own mother and her beloved Huldah, but as she embraced Tirzah, tears streamed down her cheeks.

"Lapidoth, if only I could find Lapidoth, my husband. If only I knew he had not been killed," sobbed Deborah burying her face on Huldah's small shoulder.

"Don't cry, Deborah. Please, don't cry," comforted the dark-haired child putting her arms lovingly about the waist of her older sister.

Tirzah, herself, rejoicing in the reunion with her oldest daughter, was confused by the tears of the girl whom she had heard was now such a "judge" and "holy woman" of the tribe of Ephraim.

"They called you a 'judge,' Deborah," said Tirzah bewildered, "yet now you seem no different from my own daughter in our days in the tents near Mount Ephraim. I cannot understand it."

"Yes, Deborah," added Huldah excitedly, "You must be much different now!"

"I am the same person, Huldah. I am still your daughter, Mother. What I did was just one deed of strength, my one gift to you and our people and our God."

"You were very strong and very brave, Deborah," said Benjamin loyally as he stood by Miriam at the doorway of the tent.

"I am not brave now," cried Deborah. "I am only a woman terribly frightened for her husband's life. The battle is over now. I want only to go back home with Lapidoth."

"Deborah! Deborah!"

No one could mistake the gruff voice of Barak.

"Come, Deborah. There is still work to be done. Sisera has not yet been captured. Come, Deborah, come and search for the Canaanite captain."

In utter fatigue Deborah moved outside the tent.

"I can do nothing more, Barak. I have already done all that you asked. I have led the armies. I have fought and prayed for our victory, but now I am tired, so very, very tired. Please, Barak, I cannot search for Sisera now. I must sleep. . . ."

"You need not search for Sisera!"

Barak and Deborah turned immediately at the sound of the voice behind them.

"Jael!"

"Jael, is it really you?"

Deborah threw her arms about the young girl before her. "It is I, Deborah. I am the girl you so lovingly befriended. I told you I should never forget you."

"But, Jael, wasn't it you by the well when we first camped here? You seemed then to have forgotten me altogether."

"It was I, Deborah. I was there, but I could not speak to you, for Heber the Kenite, my husband, would have seen us together. Had he known of our friendship, I might never have been able to have brought you this gift today."

As she said this, Jael drew forth from her cloak a long dagger set with many jewels in its handle.

"It is the knife of Sisera!" gasped Barak. "Where did you get it? Tell me quickly that I may kill that enemy of the Hebrews."

"You cannot kill Sisera," replied Jael.

"Not kill him!" stormed Barak. "He has oppressed my tribesmen, murdered my people, and now, like a coward, has crept away from the battle. Who dares to say I cannot kill such a man?"

"You cannot kill Sisera," answered Jael calmly, "for I have already slain him."

"*You!* How could a small woman like you kill such a fierce warrior? You must have been dreaming this night!" retorted Barak.

Looking again at the dagger, however, his voice became less certain when he asked, "How then, Jael? How *could* you do such a thing?"

"You know well, Barak, what a treacherous man my husband is. Always Heber is known for spying upon one army and then upon the other."

Then looking quickly and lovingly at Deborah, Jael added, "I did not know such things, however, when he so pleasingly invited me to leave the caravan and enter his tent after we had set out from Ramah. He seemed kindly then, but each day I saw his craftiness become more shrewd and cunning, and his treachery more devious."

"Then that is why you pretended not to know me by the well," exclaimed Deborah.

"Yes, for lately he has been selling most of his secrets and information to Jabin or Sisera. Even yesterday Sisera knew that our sprawling tent had been pitched near the Kishon, so it was to our tent that Sisera ran when he saw the torrents of water coming over the chariots and all of his troops drowning or being slain before him."

"Yes, and when he saw me coming to kill him!" added Barak grimly.

"But were you not frightened, Jael, when you saw Sisera coming to your tent?" asked Deborah.

"Yes, I *was* terrified, just as you must also have been afraid when you saw the Canaanites mounted before you. But at that very moment I remembered the days with you and Lapidoth, Deborah. I remembered the songs and stories you sang about our people and how much you loved them and wanted us to be victorious. I remembered also my vow to you that one day I would show you my love and loyalty.

"So when Sisera approached our tent, even though my husband Heber had been gone all during the day, and even though my heart quaked with fear, I invited the Canaanite leader inside."

"And Sisera was in your tent as I pursued him all the way to Harosheth!" roared Barak.

"Yes," answered Jael. "Come and see."

"I was very courteous and hospitable to the weary Sisera and he had no reason to distrust me, since it was my husband who sold him so many secrets about the Hebrew plans.

"I invited him into our tent and gave him a mat to lie down upon and I even covered him with Heber's best robe. Sisera was very glad to hide, and when he asked for a drink of water, I brought him some of our best milk.

"It was when he had fallen asleep that I knew what I must do. At first I had no plan, but I took a tent peg in my hand and a hammer also. Standing over him, thinking of all the Hebrews whom Sisera had killed and of all the Israelites he had bound into slavery, and of all our land he had taken away, it was suddenly for you, Deborah, and for all our people, and for Yahweh also, that I raised the hammer and brought it down, driving the tent peg through the head of Sisera. He is dead now, Deborah. I have kept my vow to you and to the Lord."

"I must see this thing," cried Barak astounded. "How could a young woman like you kill the great Sisera?"

But then Barak looked at Deborah and the trace of a smile crossed his gruff features. "There is only one other woman who could do such a deed for her people. It was that woman, Deborah, who told me that Sisera would not be given into my hand. How very strange that the mighty Lord would use *women* for such deeds as have been accomplished. I cannot understand it. I cannot comprehend such things.

"But about this last, I want to know more. Come, Jael, come and show me the tent and the place where Sisera died."

Barak turned, and for the second time in his life, followed a woman as Jael led him toward the Kenite tent.

Deborah remained by her own tent. The battle had been successful and victory was theirs.

As her thoughts turned to Lapidoth she raised her eyes and saw coming toward her a soldier of Ephraim covered with the mud of the turbulent Kishon.

"Lapidoth!" shouted Deborah, running toward her husband.

"It's all right now, Deborah. It's all right. The battle is over now and again we are together."

"We are together indeed," cried Deborah as she felt her husband's arms close about her tired body.

"Your work is over, Deborah. You can now be simply a woman of Ephraim. You who have been a "judge" can now be my wife; we shall have the children we have longed for."

"Yes," answered Deborah leaning wearily upon Lapidoth, "Asahiah will never see the sons that I shall bear you nor the daughters eitner, but now surely I shall become a 'mother of Israel.' "

The sun was now coming forth and beginning to dry up the tumultuous Kishon, and the chariots were lying broken and forgotten in the mud.

Grateful for the sunshine and the warmth of the noonday, rejoicing in the sure love of her husband and her people, Deborah breathed a final prayer as the Judge of Israel: "So let all thine enemies perish, O Lord: but let them that love him be as the sun when he goeth forth in his might."

And the land had rest forty years.

The Deborah of this story lived over 3000 years ago, but her life was as fascinating, challenging, and ultimately rewarding as that of any woman living in the twentieth century.

Mrs. Hogan has drawn a sharp portrait of the young girl who dreamed dreams, worried over her appearance, fell in love as girls do everywhere, and matured into a woman who led her people to victorious battle against the Canaanites.

Based on material in the fourth and fifth chapters of *Judges,* the story elaborates on biblical incidents of Deborah's courtship by Lapidoth, her reign as the "holy woman of Israel," the loss of her firstborn child, and the decision to go into battle with Barak.

The author provides the reader with an accurate account of the background, customs, and beliefs of the Hebrew people of Old Testament times in an excellent fictional biography.